A Portrait of Lord Shree Krishna

Rupa Goswami

MAPLE
PUBLISHERS

A Portrait of Lord Shree Krishna

English translation © 2023 by Arjundas Adhikari

First Published in 2023

ISBN 978-1-915996-98-5 (Paperback)
    978-1-915996-99-2 (E-Book)

Book cover and Book layout by:

White Magic Studios
www.whitemagicstudios.co.uk

Published by:

Maple Publishers

Fairbourne Drive, Atterbury,
Milton Keynes,
MK10 9RG, UK
www.maplepublishers.com

The back cover image is a gunja berry necklace, the kind that Radharani enjoys making for Shree Krishna.

A CIP catalogue record for this title is available from the British Library.

Contents

RUPA GOSWAMI

A PORTRAIT OF LORD SHREE KRISHNA
A drama in seven acts

TRANSLATED FROM THE SANSKRIT
BY ARJUNDAS ADHIKARI

INTRODUCTION.

Written in 1532 CE, the same period as Martin Luther, and just prior to colonial rule in India, *A Portrait of Lord Shree Krishna,* (for which the Sanskrit is *Vidagdha Madhava*) is a romantic drama, retelling the youth-hood of Lord Shree Krishna, the favourite divinity of the Indian sub-continent, who lived in Uttar Pradesh c. 1000 BCE, or earlier.

1. RUPA GOSWAMI

Rupa Goswami was born into a scholarly brahman family in Bengal in 1489 CE. He became learned in Sanskrit, Arabic and Persian, and was enlisted as chief secretary to sultan Alauddin Husein Shah, whereupon he found himself shunned outright by the orthodox Hindu community. On meeting the charismatic Shree Chaitanya in 1514 CE, however, he was inspired to give up his government position, and he became an ardent devotee of Shree Krishna. Rupa Goswami's writings are many, and *A Portrait of Lord Shree Krishna* is the first of two plays written at the behest of the illustrious Chaitanya. Rupa Goswami passed over in 1564 CE.

2. THE IMPORTANCE OF SHREE KRISHNA TODAY

It is well worth a look at some of the ways in which the phenomenon of Shree Krishna bears relevance to today, beginning with His role as divine vigilante, relieving the earth-goddess of the burden of being exploited by the largely irresponsible leaders of the time. The impact of the exploitation of the earth by corporate greed on its wholesome condition today, would also appear to warrant heroic activism to set it right, on the part of the conscientious. The backdrop of the play is the luxuriant, exotic Forest of Vrindavan flourishing under the care of its eponymous overseer, Vrindadevi, and the story conveys a fond regard for nature as the true resource of value. Metaphors for beauty consistently employ the excellences of natural phenomena, such as luminaries, forest-flowers, scents, lightening, clouds, deer, sunset, water, etc.

Regarding *ahimsa*, or non-violence, Krishna's realm, Vrindavan, is a micro-kingdom in which the main source of livelihood is cow-keeping, where the idea of cow-slaughter is completely unheard of. The prosperities freely afforded by cow and bull, such as milk, milk-products, agricultural power and fertilizer, engender a deep appreciation from the cow-folk, and to kill their gentle benefactors for their meat would never be tolerated.

The dominant theme of the drama, whilst unorthodox, gives a clear vision of the dramatic power-play between fabulous blue-blackish Shree Krishna, and the fabulous cowherd girls of His village. The give and take is shared, but predisposes in favour of the cowherd girls. Krishna is a great hero, defending His kingdom against formidable antagonists, but He Himself is governed by the love of Shrimati Radharani. Radharani's epithet *Madana-mohana-mohini*, lauds Her as the 'Enchantress of the enchanter of Cupid.' The narrative comprises a timeless exposition of power-sharing among genders.

Rupa Goswami's celebrated detachment from worldly affairs - he owned literally nothing more than a water pot and a waistcloth - is attributed to his great devotion to Krishna. Indeed, meditation on Krishna, Krishna's insights, and the directives upheld by Him, is common practise among those seeking transcendence, and millions regard it not only as a profoundly spiritual affair, but as the easiest, most effective path to mindfulness. A recent newspaper article in which the last surviving member of Hilary and Tenzing's Everest expedition expressed anxiety about lack of snow on Mount Everest, reminded me of Krishna's statement in *Bhagavad-gita*: 'Of immovable things I am the Himalayas.' Likewise, the, 'Now I am become Death, the destroyer of the worlds,' quote, used by Robert Oppenheimer when he first witnessed the detonation of the atomic bomb, is also derived from Krishna's *Bhagavad-gita*. No one can argue that Krishna's claims are not arresting and altogether extraordinary.

3. SANSKRIT DRAMA.

A Portrait of Lord Shree Krishna follows the structure of a 'Comprehensive Play,' or *maha-nataka,* as delineated in sage Bharata's handbook to dramaturgy, known as the *Natyashastra,* compiled in the 1st century CE. The main source of reference for this translation is Vishvanatha Chaktravartin's invaluable commentary, *Vidagdha-madhava-vivriti.*

In his introduction to Oxford World's Classics' English edition of the drama *The Recognition of Shakuntala,* by Kalidas, Dr. WJ Johnson advocates a performance-based approach to translating Sanskrit drama: 'The fact that Kalidas was also a great poet should not seduce us into treating his plays as simply anthologies of poetry ... [his works] like those of any other great playwright only come alive on stage: the words on the page are the beginning of the process, not its culmination. This is even more the case when they have been translated into another language.' Professor Arthur Berriedale Keith comments in a similar way in his definitive work on the genre, 'The Sanskrit drama ... despite its complexity, is essentially intended for performance, nor is there the slightest doubt that the early dramatists were anything but composers of plays meant only to be read. They were connoisseurs, we may be certain, in the merits which would accrue to their works from the accessories of the dance, music, song, and the attractions of acting.'[1]

With this in mind, this rendering of *A Portrait of Lord Shree Krishna*, while performance-oriented, aspires to be true to the original flavours of a unique and relatively unexplored area of classical drama.

---

1 Arthur Berriedale Keith, *The Sanskrit Drama, its Origin, Development, Theory and Practice*, 358

DRAMATIS PERSONAE.

NANDA MAHARAJA, king of Vrindavan.
LORD SHREE KRISHNA, son of Nanda.
BALARAMA, son of Nanda.
MADHUMANGALA, brahman boy.
SUBAL, cowherd boy.
SHRIDAMA, cowherd boy.
ABHIMANYU, cow-lord.
RUPA GOSWAMI, play's author.
STAGE MANAGER

YASHODA, queen of Vrindavan.
PAURNAMASI, wise-lady of Vrindavan.
SHRIMATI RADHARANI, 'bride' of Abhimanyu.
LALITA, handmaid to Radharani.
VISHAKHA, handmaid to Radharani.
CHANDRAVALI, cowherd girl.
PADMA, handmaid to Chandravali.
SHAIVYA, handmaid to Chandravali.
NANDIMUKHI, cowherd girl.
SARANGI, cowherd girl.
VRINDA, guardian of the forest.
JATILA, Abhimanyu's mother.
MUKHARA, Radharani's grandmother.
KARALA, Chandravali's grandmother.

Kakhati (a female monkey), Rangini (Radha's pet), Suranga (Krishna's pet), Maina Bird, Parrot.

SCENE: *Vrindavan: India.*

EULOGIUM.

Come celebrate a wonder that can mitigate life's woes,
A draught of fabled nectar of the kind that heaven knows,
That all may come to know - that is available for free -
The magic of the love between Krishna and Radharani!

Bounds of Radharani's love so transcend any limit,
That Krishna once embraced Her mood to try and
comprehend it,
Incarnating incognito - as the Golden Avatar -
May He also enter in your heart - jai Sachi-nandana!

PROLOGUE.

Rupa G. And now, straight to the point, kind ladies and kind gentlemen -
Point being, the commission that the good Lord Shiva's given:
Was in a dream he came to order me - said he - 'Director!
In this forest of Vrindavan – by the ghat, 'longside the river,
Please note there has arrived a very focussed coalition -
Who've journeyed to the forests here in long-standing tradition -
Upheld by all devotees of the darling boy of Nanda -
Nanda Maharaja's son - the Supreme Lord Shree Krishna:
He who's the complexion of dark rain-clouds rumbling thunder;
Known to all the cowherd girls as Kanha, or, Kanhaiya;
In whom those gopis' hearts play just like dolphins in the sea;
The unequalled professor of flute-playing mastery;
The gem-like youth, who's fragrance never fails to fascinate;
More charming than a dove in an intoxicated state;
Who revelled in these groves here on the banks of the Yamuna,

Beside the hill of Govardhan, in ways that conjure wonder!
'But,' said he, 'how're they to cope? Who'll bring these pilgrims cheer?
The woods the gopis searched when Krishna disappeared, are here!
The river banks where all the gopis danced with Him, are there!
Such recollections make pure pilgrims miss Him, in despair!
It's down to you - I give you all the blessings that you need!
To spare them, you present your show, sir! So – do please proceed!'
So here we are - to execute the great Shiva's desire ...

Enter STAGE MANAGER.

Stage M. Indeed we are! The actors are in character – on fire!
Just give the word! To start, it's to the author we defer!
Sir, bless us to begin your play – Portrait of Lord Shree Krishna!

Rupa G. Alright, dear troubadour – alright. They're dressed – they're ready, eh?
[*Reflects.*] First off, I will confess – though, not refined poetically -
As the theme's Shree Krishna, and you're pilgrims of discretion;
I'm confident that from it you'll derive due satisfaction -
If well-water's been sanctified, it's sipped as it were nectar!

Stage M. And will you please recite the prayers to bless our little theatre!
The gods could well be critiqued by this clever audience;
And being humble actors, best to give ourselves a chance!

Rupa G. Sir, who have we before us? Please do properly appraise!

They have very cultured backgrounds, but have very modest ways;
They put themselves last and give encouragement to others;
In that way they're munificent - and big praise gives them shudders.
[*Beholding the audience, he smiles amicably.*] Sagacious devotees of Krishna – do not take offence;
The actor wasn't thinking – but his good-will is immense!
[*Bows.*] Not hard to recognise I am not really qualified,
But, absorption in Shree Krishna is accepted far and wide,
As the springboard to perfection, so we proceed confidently -
Who cares who lights the fire in the gold refinery?
With a humble bit of stagecraft, may the dear Lord be conveyed!
[*Folds hands in prayer.*] Vrindavan Forest groves, that's where our master's always stayed;
Vrindavan is the place in which He permanently glows;
With a glimpse of Him in person, the desire to please Him follows!

    Stage M. I have prayed for such a chance – all of my Diwalis at once!
A stage beside the forest groves, and what an audience!
A play about the famous cowherdesses' divine charmer;
Let us begin the delectable acts of said new drama!

    Rupa G. Shame it is, some can't relate. It is, though, troubadour;
Feel sorry for them – makes you stop and wonder, that's for sure...

    Stage M. Yes, when you consider your accomplished artistry;
It's just that there are some who can't relate to quality -
Clever cuckoos are in heaven when they reach a mango tree,

The camels, bless them, walk straight past, plod by indifferently.
Let's delight the hearts of all the clever cuckoos here -
With this drama that's descended from the spiritual sphere!

Rupa G. Bless me, sir – Paurnamasi! This is quite extraordinary!
She's behind the trysts between Krishna and Radharani!
Spring, it was. Shree Krishna's mind was turned to thoughts of love;
This marvellous, good lady knew who He was thinking of!

Paurna. [*Off-stage.*] I see you've my great secret in your drama, good director
I don't know how you know, but, I admit you are correct, sir -
Was going to arrange that Radha meets with Lord Shree Krishna!

Rupa G. [*Surprised, turns to the wings.*] Paurnamasi has returned! Well, bless my soul – you see her?
Imposing as the mother goddess – shining in a sari;
Beautiful white locks – behold, the Ma of Sandipani!
From Nanda's house, she's stepping out - with adjutant in tow,
Shree Narada's disciple, dressed and ready for the show!

[*Exeunt Rupa Goswami and Stage Manager.*

Gokoola Village, near Nanda Maharaja's house. Morning.
Enter PAURNAMASI *and* NANDIMUKHI.

Paurna. I see you've my great secret in your drama, good director;
I don't know how you know, but, I admit you are correct, sir -

I'm going to arrange that Radha meets with Lord Shree Krishna!
And, Nandimukhi, child – he makes me feel a whole lot better!
Nice to hear enthusiasm – nice, that theatrician.

Nandi. How's it going, noble lady?

Paurna. Oh, I know, it's slow progression;
We'll get there, young lady, I'm just waiting for a chance;
Their meeting is the mission and we're going to go the distance

Nandi. Why did you have Radhika leave the village? Leave Gokoola?
Had Her hiding in Santanu – how's She s'posed to meet Kanhaiya?

Paurna. I do have to be cautious 'bout the threat of evil Kamsa.

Nandi. What threat, noble lady? How's the king know 'bout Radhika?

Paurna. For the simple fact that Radharani is a marvel!
A marvel's not concealable – of marvels, news will travel;
If one wears musk, for instance - everybody knows it's on you.

Nandi. But, really – you've let Radha become lost to Abhimanyu!
Let grandmother Mukhara give him Radhika for marriage!
Soon as She got back, they did the marriage in the village!
Far as I know, Radha's heart's the property of Krishna,
And, noble lady, you don't mind? I see your mood is brighter!

Paurna. It is. And I've a reason for it.

Nandi. Mystery to me!

Paurna. [*Smiling.*] No marriage! Got to tell you, child, that that was fakery!

Krishna has a sorceress – there's no one she can't fool!

Nandi. [*Delighted.*] I see what you've done - Radhika's safe now in Gokool?

Paurna. Long as She *looks* married, Kamsa-trouble looms much less!
But Abhimanyu's character's a new unpleasantness.

Nandi. Oh...?

Paurna. Jealous that fair cowherd girls are all so fond of Krishna;
He wants to take Radhika far away and isolate Her!

Nandi. Can't Krishna's sorceress do something?

Paurna. Could if I could reach her,
Her movements aren't predictable - I can't really involve her.

Nandi. Isn't there another way to keep the man in check?

Paurna. Well, yes - he does respond to sweet-talk - poor chap is myopic;
I'll hold him for a while – he's quite disposed to flattery.

Nandi. [*Encouraged.*] Has Govardhan said anything? That Kamsa-man should worry;
His fair wife, Chandravali, is so *very* fond of Krishna!

Paurna. One does imagine that he would, but he, it seems, knows better;
Overlooking something there.

Nandi. But she's obsessed with Krishna!

Paurna. No stopping her, my dear – and she did not need me to help her.

Nandi. No stopping you, good lady - since the day Kanhaiya was born,
You've been right here, watched over Him - now, when did your love dawn?
We all know your homeland is a long way from Gokoola.

Paurna. For that, child, I'm indebted to my kind spiritual master!

Nandi. And, then there is your son - he understands the situation?

Paurna. Oh, yes! He sent his own son who is splendid for the mission!
My grandson Madhumangala – resourceful boy, as well.

Nandi. And a fine time he is having, it is quite easy to tell;
Because of you Madhu's becoming very dear to Krishna.

Paurna. The whole point is, we all make sure that Radha falls for Krishna;
That's your job too, my dear!

Nandi.   [*Delighted.*] But She is enamoured already;
She adores Kanhaiya – with a passion, noble lady!

Paurna. How d'you know?

Nandi.   Why, when She hears Krishna-Kanhaiya's name -
Her hair's on end - exalting in it - every time's the same!

Paurna. It's always true - the name of Krishna does have that effect;
Two syllables - how heavenly! Quite natural, I suspect -
To want them sounded so, that just one mouth becomes too few -
To hear them, and be thinking how a million ears might do;
To find that you've that name, and nothing else, inside the heart!

Nandi. Is love for Krishna something that our temple-gods impart?
Radha at the Sun-shrine with Lalita and Vishakha;
Chandravali at Durga's with her friends Padma and Shaivya?

Paurna. The way those darlings love is quite inherent - nothing less!
Tradition's all it is that calls them all to temple service.
    Nandi. While Radha-love's amazing - her two friends make it redouble.
    Paurna. Precisely. Now, my dear – it's time we moved things on a little!
I want a portrait done of Krishna, specially, for Radha;
That Vishakha's good at painting, so the task should go to her.
    Nandi. Alright, good lady.
    Paurna.   I am going to go and prompt Shree Krishna;
Easy – all it takes is but a mention of Radhika.
I've laddus ready – my excuse to meet Him in the forest.
    Nandi. He's off there now, He's going – look! Two parents looking stressed!
Poor Nanda and Yashoda miss Kanhaiya readily;
No holding back - you see? His friends all joining Him, good lady!
Brother Balaraam, Madhu, Shridam, and all the rest;
Farewells to the village, and it's down towards the forest!
    Paurna. [*Observing contentedly.*] My, but He stands out, does Krishna - shining like a gem!
Flower-adorned, with presence like a god from heaven's kingdom!
Goodness me, a portrait - what breath-taking lotus-eyes!
Robed in yellows, sharp as any fresh-made saffron dyes!
I'm off to go and get some sweets - you go and find Vishakha!

                      [Exeunt Paurnamasi and Nandimukhi.

ACT I.

Magic Flute.

Outskirts of Gokoola.
Enter KRISHNA, NANDA MAHARAJA, YASHODA,
MADHUMANGALA, BALARAMA, SUBAL *and* SHRIDAMA.

Krishna. [*Surveying His herd of cows with satisfaction.*]
Could be the holy Ganges going to join Vrindavan's river -
All gleaming - crystal-white, a steady flow of bovine vigour!
Very thirsty cows...

Nanda M.   Oh, yes - now, turn around, my son...
                                    [*Krishna turns.*
We cowherd folk are lucky – look, as far as the horizon!
Great cow-pens nestling among trees, lush forest pressing in;
From Mount Govardhan to Kal'ya Lake, our bonny hamlet thriving!

Krishna. Madhumangal, friend, seems like My father's come too far;
Should be getting back to Gokool – the same goes for you, Mama.

Yasho. You forget the village every afternoon, my son;
And every meal gets cold – and after all the work I've done!

Madhu. My Queen, by the cows, I swear that's not His fault! Here's why:

                          [*Krishna regards him appreciatively.*

There's things going on that decent persons would decry;
Coerced, He is – dragged in the groves – for what? For fun and play!
And, I'll tell you who's to ... [*Breaks off.*

Krishna. [*Embarrassed. Aside.*] Imbecile! He'll give the game away!
Don't let on about the gopis, fool!

[*Gives Madhumangala a forbidding shake of the head.*
Madhu.   Sakhe? Is something wrong?
The good lady ought to know, no doubt she will before too long.

Krishna. [*Aside.*] Good grief! What a disastrous liability is he!

Madhu. Kanhaiya cuts it short, though, with those cowherd boys, dear lady...

Krishna. [*Amused. Aside.*] Now why did I presume he'd something else to say in mind?

Yasho. Fact, Madhu, dear, Lalita said those boys were being unkind;
Girls did say they're hindering them, frivolous, and so on.

Nanda. My dear, which Gokool girl would be the one to wed our son?

Yasho. At the moment, He's still milk-mouthed, dear – our boy's still much too young!

Madhu. [*Aside to Krishna.*] Of course You're milk-mouthed, friend, for that is what the gopis thrive on;
A thousand thirsty gopis have Your helpful mouth to drink from!

[*Krishna smiles.*

Nanda M. Your mother's who she is, Krishna – she does get overcome;
Besotted with You, handsome – cannot help herself, my son -

And You can clearly see, milk's drenched the blouse that she has on!
[*Hugs Krishna.*] Liniment and lotus, sandal, moon and eclipsed sun;
All cooling – yes – but hugging You, their cooling-worth seems gone...

    Krishna. Cows are very hungry, father. Stopping. Peering back;
I think you should be going now.

    Nanda M.   My son – we shall backtrack!

               [*Exeunt Nanda Maharaja and Yashoda.*

    Krishna. [*Looking ahead.*] That's a lot of nectar oozing from the ripened mangos -
Drives the bees so crazy, they don't know what comes or goes!
Ah - the cool caress of the Malayan mountain breezes,
Swaying vernal paradise - no other place so pleases!

    Bal. Very sacred here, Shridam, it so gives that impression;
Pretty flowers inspire the bees to get themselves religion;
That's holy-hummimg, that – just like the clergy when they pray!

    Krishna. Vrindavan Forest likes the flute, Madhu, and so, I play.

                  [*Raises flute to His lips.*

    Bal. [*Taken aback.*] Ah, yes – now I'm confused - normality has lost it's way;
Hard things melt, and running water's slowing and won't go;
Trees sway in time before your eyes – and just go with the flow!
There it is – flute-melodist's exceptional as ever!
Bets are off about the chaos that His music will deliver!

Madhu. Amazing notes – look at the cows - their situation's helpless;
Soaking flowers in milk – my, are they lost in happiness!
[*Leaning on Krishna.*] The flute deserves the credit, friend, try not to be so proud;
You had Your part to play, of course – but, false pride's not allowed!

[*Murmuring in the sky.*

Sage N. [*Off-stage.*] The clouds don't move – celestial singer's stunned and paralysed!
Great sages' meditations fractured - Brahma's hypnotised!
What's impassioned divine Bali? seized the divine Snake-Lord's soul?
What has cracked the cosmic lining? 'Tis the flute makes heaven roll!

Bal. [*Astonished, looks up. Aside.*] Heaven's bard is on his lute! That's him up in his cloud ...

Madhu. [*Horrified.*] Run for it! Help! Save yourselves!
Shrid.   Plain crazy - and too loud!
Madhu. [*Continuing, aghast.*] Half-wit cowherd, look! That demon flying on a swan!
Four-heads! Ye gads! And one with snakes – great ghoul with nothing on!
[*Trembling.*] It's bedlam in the skies - led by the one with all the eyes;
King Kamsa's on the war-path - he's enlisting vicious allies!

[*Terrified, he ducks behind Krishna.*

Krishna. [*Aside.*] Flute's drawn the gods - all diving down - immersing in the cloud!

[*Plays flute.*

Madhu. [*Invigorated. Aside.*] Bold salvo from my friend to tranquilise the monstrous crowd;
He's totally subdued them – what a maestro! I'm alive!

[*Struts about.*] __Now then, you demons! Understand from me - you won't survive!

With mantra-power, and deadly bow, I'll dash your silly pates! [*Raises his staff, bounds around.*

Bal. [*Amused.*] Go easy, friend – it's Shiva and Brahma – high-heaven's greats;

Lord Indra's on the left, there, with the other shining ones.

Madhu. [*Well relieved.*] Can't you tell when I'm joking? No? I didn't think they're demons!

You actually believed me! You were wondering when to bolt!

Krishna. [*Smiles.*] Always others who're impulsive, never you, My faithful dolt.

Bal. He's savouring the tune – look - Brahma's swaying on his swan;

The flute's bewitched all his eight ears, to lose him his decorum!

[*Lute music.*

Sage N. [*Off-stage.*] The oceanic Shiva is in thrall to Krishna's tune,

Spring-tide emotion impelled by the lyric Krishna-Moon!

Bal. Lord Indra weeps a deluge - from a thousand eyes he cries;

A shower, a downpour – it's no cloud - we're drenched by Indra's eyes!

The melody's moved heaven's king to melt in great devotion.

Krishna. [*Aside.*] Thing is, I'm not that inclined to ancient lords of heaven;

It's what it is.

[*Krishna and His friends enter Vrindavan Forest.*

__Now, this place, Madhu's, what you call a forest! Exquisite flowers - note how the air's in jasmine perfume dressed!

Bee-serenades, the juice of pomegranates flowing freely;
A feast for every single sense - divine prosperity!

 Madhu. Not so impressed myself, my friend – too many pesky bees;
Good fun for me's Your mother's cooking - never fails to please.

 Krishna. These woods yield everything, My friend - old climbers here, for instance;
Yield anything you'd care to want!

 Madhu.   They do? I'll take the chance.
You always speak the truth, I've heard, that is what most folk say;
So, let us see. [*Folds hands in prayer.*] Dear vines – to you, I, Madhumangal, pray:
Please give me some candies, as my friend is very hungry!

Enter PAURNAMASI, sweets in hand.

 Paurna. Ah – handsome one – some sweets for You – I know You'll find them tasty!
 Bal. [*Smiling.*] A generous old vine, my friend!
 Paurna.   A cowherdess, Bal'raam!
But, many say she's generous.
 Krishna.   Which cowherd lady's that, ma'am?
 Paurna. It's Mukhara, my handsome!
 Krishna.   What a very nice surprise!
And, why's she sending laddus out?
 Paurna.   She wants to advertise -
The marriage of her granddaughter to master Abhimanyu!
 Krishna. Which granddaughter?
 Paurna.   Which? Radhika – a first-class wedding, too!

Krishna. [*Spellbound. Aside.*] The one My mother talks about with fervent admiration [*Becomes self-conscious.*

Paurna. [*Aside.*] Raam's sidled off politely seeing Krishna's sharp reaction...

Krishna. [*Aside.*] I've got to change the subject quick - can't let My feelings go.

__Won't you take some flowers? A day for turning out well, no?

These lovely vines are stuffed with blooms.

Paurna. [*Smiling.*] Well, here's the lucky thing -

Today, these are the very blooms the gopis *will* be seeking; Which means, my lad, fate's handing You an opportune occasion!

Krishna. [*Smiling, with a questioning look.*] What do you mean, good woman?

Paurna. [*Amused.*] Now, don't get me wrong, young man;

I mention it because it means the gopis shan't be in - That's butter stocks alone at home and asking to be taken!

Krishna. I see, alright – but, look, truth is, that they're not good to Me!

When they come here pulling flowers, it's vandalism. Really!

They manhandle the creepers - I won't give permission - sorry.

Paurna. The gopis pick the vine-flowers, my dear boy, because You wear them;

That's what it's about - I don't see why You'd want deter them.

Krishna. [*Smiling.*] You say that, but where they're concerned, your dealings all slide sidelong;

Keep sticking up for cowherd girls who're always in the wrong!

Paurna. Handsome, Radha and the gopis aren't mischievous - not at all!
They zealously pick flowers You like – they're fond of You, that's all.

Krishna. [*Aside.*] Keeps on mentioning Her name - can't get away from Radha.

Madhu. [*Aside.*] Pressed His buttons - Radha's name – poor boy's at sea with ardour.
___No need to be so anxious, friend!

Krishna.   [*Apparently irritated.*] Not anxious, lively brother!

Madhu. The candy's yours – I do assure You!

Krishna.   That's laddu – not candy!

Madhu. [*Laughing.*] Sakhe – it isn't me who talk of Radha's turns all funny!

Paurna. [*Aside.*] Ah - touché, young brahman-boy, it's what I came to see -
Heart gets the better of Him, and He acts up very cagey!
___Don't hanker too much, handsome, because Radha's like a star -
With You on earth, and Her on high – maybe the star's too far!

Krishna. [*Smiling, glances up. Crosses to Balarama.*] It's getting hot – we've got to get this herd to water, brother;
Take some laddus with You and enjoy them by the river.
I need to spend a little time with Shridam and Subal.

[*Exit Balarama.*

Paurna. [*Aside.*] My commissioned artwork is in need of an appraisal.

[*Passing Krishna with a smile, she heads off.*

Krishna. [*Takes a step and stops.*] Shridama, My dear friend – d'you realise no one's like Radhika?

[*Shridama lowers his head.*

Sub. You can't ask that of him, dear friend - You're talking to Her brother!

Krishna. That is true – right, here's our spot – the grove of burflower trees -
A tune or two will drive away the Radha-blues with ease...

> [*Exeunt Krishna, Madhumangala, Subal and Shridama.*

Paurna. [*Walks, comes across Radha.*] So, here She is - my Radha, and another lively sakhi.
[*Concealed.*] Gold is not as radiant, nor as bright as Radharani!
Lilies not as pretty as her eyes ... why, She's so fair –
A set of fresh new blooming lotus flowers don't compare!
I'll leave them to their banter - take the wood-path to Vishakha.

> [*Exit.*

Enter RADHA *and* LALITA, *searching for gunja berries.*

Radha. What's my mother-in-law up to over there, sakhi Lalita?

Lal. Worship. That's the altar where she does her puja, sakhi,
Does the Sun-god worship underneath the tamal tree.

Radha. [*With keen curiosity.*] You've often said, of many forests – this one is the best.
How true it is, Lalita – a delight, is Vrinda Forest!

Lal. Indeed, my friend – I like to call it Krishna's leisure-garden.

Radha. [*Uneasy. Aside.*] Oh, I do love the name! __ Sakhi, it's whose? Who's that again?

Lal. [*Insouciant smile.*] Belongs to Krishna - yes, young lady.

Radha. [*Aside.*] Takes your breath away!

What's He like in person? [*Acting normal.*] __Sakhi, let's ...
get underway:
This grove is full of gunja berries
      Lal.   [*Jovially.*] Alright, but take care -
You're very pretty - need to worry who it is that's in there!
Just might be the renegade who frequents all the bowers!
The swarthy prince, who sweeps girls up, and takes them
all as lovers!
      Radha. [*Hesitant, returning a good-humoured smile.*]
Well, you should know – believe He swept you up, Lalita
sakhi.
      Lal. [*Laughs.*] Why'd He have bothered Me, friend? I
don't have Your kind of beauty!
                                        [*Flute music.*
      Radha. [*Enthralled. Aside.*] Oh, hair-raising sound!
                                        [*Loses composure.*
      Lal.   [*Observing her. Aside.*] And, that is called,
'deer-caught-in-snare.'
      Radha. [*Trying to compose Herself. Aside.*] Who is this
whose playing can send nectar into air?
      Lal. [*Nearing.*] I think You trust me, Radharani. Do
You? Do You trust me?
      Radha. I do! Don't have to ask that, as I trust implicitly.
      Lal. Well, You really got distracted, sakhi – sure that
You're alright?
      Radha. [*Abashed.*] That music isn't safe, I feel that
something's not gone right;
I do not know what it's about - it puts Me in a state;
And not a state for decent folk, whose moral fibre's straight,
Odious state, sakhi!
      Lal.   Oh, but, they're darling songs, dear thing!
      Radha. [*Restless.*] Look – I know what songs are – they
aren't scything, scolding - freezing!

But, I'm cut and burned and frozen– it's not nice – the fluting hurts Me!
[*Animated.*] Really mean it, sakhi – music's thoroughly bewitched Me;
Insidiously. Seriously 'bout to come unstuck...

Enter VISHAKHA, painting in hand.

Vish. [*Assessing Radha. Aside.*] Hardly recognise Her - K'nhaiya's magic playing's struck;
She's traumatised, poor thing – I think She needs some sympathy. [*Approaches.*
_Pale girl, don't cry. It's all alright. There now - You take it easy!
Shree krishna's flute has this effect, especially with You - Hairs on end!
Radha. [*Oblivious, unsteady.*] Head-over-heels, Lalita - each time too!
Lal. I know, sakhi - the music from the river-side is potent!
Tormenting as the Bird-King is tormenting to a serpent;
Like a cure for the demure from a celestial physician;
The sound of pride in virtue ending up merely a notion!
Radha. I'm feeling very strange, My friend. I think I might lie down...
Vish. Radhika, My dear friend – may I dissipate Your frown?
In my hand I have something to cheer You up again.
Radha. So, let us see, Vishakha – we have here a leafy den.

[Exeunt.

ACT II.

Love Letter.

Gokoola Village, near Mukhara's house. Afternoon.
Enter NANDIMUKHI.

Nandi. [*Walking.*] Not well – that's all that Paurnamasi had to say about Her...
'Nandi,' says she, 'I need to know what ails my girl Radhika!'
Not sure where to start, but there is one knows where to find Her;
I'm heading for Her grandmother Mukhara's house near here...
[*Comes across Mukhara.*] What's wrong with Mukhara! Gracious, what's all the commotion?

Enter MUKHARA.

Mukha. When's it stop? Merciless fate – goes on! Why's it go on?
Nandi. Oh, dear Mukhara! Oh, now, please, what's all the crying for?
Mukha. [*Sees Nandimukhi.*] Oh, child! Radhika's very ill!
Nandi. How's Radha ill? Say more!
Mukha. Absolutely mad, child, I can't understand Her pleas!

'Don't spoil My garland, rogue!' like that – but, She's
addressing bees!
Or, 'Please go! I'm just a girl – your banter you may keep!'
Makes no difference – none – if She's awake, if She's asleep;
The gentle girl's tormented by Her ravings day and night!

    Nandi. [*Aside.*] I'm sure She's not insane, She isn't
mad - that can't be right!
The intrigues of Kanhaiya are what must have caused
these woes.

    Mukha. Got to find the saintly lady, have to make sure
that she knows!
Child – Radha's in the palm grove, now. Go there! Watch
where She goes!

                [*Exeunt Nandimukhi and Mukhara.*

    Enter RADHA, LALITA *and* VISHAKHA.

    Radha. [*Panicking. Aside.*] I just don't understand it.
Just a portrait, and, that's all;
Again! The feelings start again - there's no let up at all!

    Lal & Vish. Radhika - dear friend, is it the change -
Your being married?
Please tell us, You are not Yourself - that's why we're
looking worried. [*Radha sighs and turns away.*

    Vish. [*Going in front of Radha.*] Something really
troubles You, dear friend - down deep within;
Why the perspiration all Your clothes are covered in?
All of Your composure lost - come on. And shudders too!
You shouldn't keep what's going on from those who care
for You!

    Radha. And not ashamed, Vishakha are you? I think
you are cruel!

    Vish. My friend - when did I cause offense? I really
don't recall!

Radha. That's pitiless - outrageous talk! Think harder, you will see!

Vish. Sakhi, try as I might, no understanding comes to me!

Radha. You're mad! How could you throw Me in a lake of blazing fire?

Vish. How's that?

Radha.   You empowered the portrait - you! And, so you did, good liar!

[*Unrestrained.*] This dark sapphire-blue ruffian here's unspeakably immodest!

He stepped out of His portrait with that feather crown of His ... [*Falters.*

Smiling. With the eyebrows dancing. That's when I was sent;

Was, at that point, it was - into the burning fire I went...

Lal. Perhaps it was a dream, friend?

Radha.   Dream? How'm I supposed to know? I'm like this when I'm sleeping and awake - it doesn't go!

It could be night or day, you see, or now - afflict Me now!

But, all shaken inside, possessed, and I do not know how,

Confounded by that sapphire-blue complexion – don't know why.

Vish. [*No idea.*] Friend, might be no more than just a flight of fantasy...

Radha. You won't accept a word! Enough! Excuses to the end!

Why're you trying to hide my failings? Shall I tell you, friend?

How, having adorned me with divers saffron cosmetics,

Underneath the burflower tree, that connoisseur of tricks!

That domineering rascal, although three times I cried, 'No!'

Dared place His arm upon Me... and smiling as He did so!

His sheer, lotus-petal blue resplendence stirred in Me,
Great eagerness for His cool touch, you see? Now do you see?
Deranged, I'd no clue where I was, or why, or even who...
[*Unhinged. Aside.*] I'm done with you, damned heart, for shame! It's three boys you're attached to!
Kanhaiya, and the flautist, *and* this dark youth - I've no pity!
I'm giving up My life, too bad - you'll soon be history!

    Lal. Merciless is springtime. Has the same effect as Cupid;
You can't avoid it, sadly, everyone is rendered stupid!

    Radha. It's good! Nice soothing mountain breezes round this time of year,
I love dove-bird songs, and droning bees, let them be near!
They stir the passions, show I am not worthy of a lifetime!

    Lal & Vish. [*In tears.*] Not true! And You're despairing without reason, without rhyme!
Nonsense! Friend, it's dark, what's going on inside Your heart.

    Radha. [*Sighing.*] What's Radha to do? Go to the doctor for My heart!
And even if I could be helped, what disgrace I'd endure!
I've made My decision, it's the way - of that I'm sure,
Hanging by this vine - My heart will stop, so there's the cure!

    Lal & Vish. [*Very uneasy.*] That's evil talk – enough! You're hurting us - do not speak more!
What You desire's available - it isn't out of reach!

    Radha. I'm lost! Radha is lost, friends! And She has no heart to teach!
You do not know, and if you did, you would not counsel Me!

    Lal & Vish. You've said it all, dear friend!

Radha.   I've not! For dreadful shame,
you see?

Lal & Vish. Shame? What shame? You're open book!
Just what is there to dread?

Radha. I fall apart after I hear Shree Krishna's name
once sounded!
Become completely mad hearing the nocturne of the flute!
Then these fixated emotions for His portrait, follow suit!
Wicked feelings for all three - don't you think I should .
die?

Lal & Vish. [*Relieved.*] So, You think a girl like You – a
gopi of Gokoola -
Could give up loving Gokool's prince in favour of another?
Gokool's prince? What - You could love some ordinary
soul?
It's talented Kanhaiya, You love - no one else at all!

Radha. [*Sigh of relief. Aside*] Love for Krishna's fine –
but things are getting out of hand...
It must be all Kanhaiya - goodness - now I understand!

Lal & Vish. Radhe, aromatic flower fragrance ventures
far and wide,
Expressly so the honey-bee gets drawn in alongside!

Re-enter NANDIMUKHI.

Nandi. [*Walking.*] Oh - here's Radha, right here.
[*Approaching.*] Good day! Hello to You, my friend!

Radha. [*Acting calm.*] Yes, hello, sakhi – how are you?

Nandi.   Well, You seem on the mend!
[*Aside.*] She does appear alright – I'll have to question Her
a bit.
__You're very young, You know, sakhi – just be aware of it;
Be no surprise if Krishna was the reason You're befuddled.

Lal. She gets the goosebumps, Nandi - just the breeze - don't get things muddled!

Nandi. [*Smiling.*] So, why's She goosebumps when we don't? You know? Don't blame the breeze!
That handsome boy could spellbind hosts of Cupids – at His ease -
To raise a brow – that's all He needs do! I know the score -
The master of the sidelong glance is prevailing once more!
Now, truthfully, when did She see the master of Gokool?

Vish. Fact is, She did.

Nandi.   You know that 'mong Your kinsmen, You're the favourite?
You run a tidy home, You please Your spouse - no doubting it;
And now the one whose habit is impressing hersdmen's wives,
Has addled You, it's true! That's made this imbalance arise!
I'll not delay, dear girl - I'm going to find us Paurnamasi!

                                             [*Exit.*

Radha. [*Pensive.*] Surrounded by religious girls, I'm devout to a tee;
Then, veering off so fast? Transgress completely. Suddenly...
[*Falters, becomes emotional.*] The sidelong look He flaunts, though, is the thing – intoxicating!
You just can't give up Gokoola's lord, the cowherd people's king.

Enter PAURNAMASI, MUKHARA, *re-enter*
NANDIMUKHI.

Paurna. So, Radha's condition, Mukhara – what are you thinking?

Mukha. Peacock plumes disturb Her. If She sees one then She shakes;
Weeping – that's the toll that spotting gunja berries takes;

This affliction, noble lady - don't know how it's come about...
A strange show-play indeed on Her heart's stage is playing out!

    Paurna. [*Aside.*] Law unto itself! The love's begun, and in full stride!
Ungovernable's what it is. __Mukhara, I'll be guide.
I've learned Mathura's king's a plan to kidnap Radharani;
Looks like he's had the girl possessed - that's pretty much the story.

    Mukha. Then what's the answer, noble lady?

    Paurna.   Prince Krishna - He's it!

    Mukha. But, Jatila's so suspicious, noble one, she'll have a fit!

    Paurna. Mukhara, tell Jatila that she doesn't have to fear,
It's my decision. Krishna's strengths are what are needed here!

                                  [*Exit Mukhara.*

[*Approaching Radha.*] May every wish You have come true in royal fashion, child!

                      [*Radha calmly returns respects.*

[*Aside.*] Our whirlwind-girl is now behaving very shy and mild;
Doesn't show She takes delight in Her inebriation;
That Maverick prince has triumphed in the stir He's set in motion;
The garden of this beauty's heart's been lost to Him, patently!
[*Whispers.*] Well, Nandi – it's a problem for Her - keeping poise - not easy;
It's epic! Love so powerful, it fiendishly unseats Her!
To cope, She has a way that contradicts Her as a lover;

Tries to forget Shree Krishna – tries to think of humdrum things;
The opposite of every honest seeker's undertakings -
Bewildered girl wants from Her heart whom yogis usher in!

Nandi. Beyond me, noble lady. Hard to take all of this in!

Paurna. That's exactly so, my child; such love-moods want explaining,
Pure poison can't effect, remotely match what She's enduring!
Pure nectar can't induce the joy that puts Her out of touch!
This beauty's love for Gokool's prince dawns in Her heart as such:
Bitter-sweet! Intensely so! It's both - delight and torment!
Now, then - shall we? Let us see. [*Approaching Radha.*] Oh, Radha! Wait a moment!
It's not like You to harbour malcontent, and be unfriendly;
The village knows Your kindness, and Your equanimity;
Your family is well-to-do, and very upper-crust;
What were You saying to your friends? Explain Your slip to us!

[*Radha demurely whispers to Lalita.*
Lal. Noble lady, Radha says your criticism hurts Her;
She has not wronged, She swears so - and good lady - you must trust Her;
She's become the victim of a rogue who holds and traps Her!
Flowers that She hurls do not deter said dark aggressor.

Paurna. [*Putting on a stern face.*] That doesn't sound to me to be a strong enough response!

Radha. [*Passionately.*] Response? I yell! He cups My mouth immediately - what chance?!

I'm frightened, try and run – He spreads His arms out -
blocks the way!
Cowering at His feet, He bites My lip distressingly!
Mother, I cannot be safe. That plume-crowned boy's so
vicious!

Paurna. [*Aside.*] Love strong as a tree, and pointless
root-hacking by us.
___Anyway, my lively girl, high time a plan's proposed -
For You to meet Your portrait-prince - and don't act ill-
disposed!
Blossom - no more scorches from these encounters of late;
What isn't good for flowers like You's a wintry freezing
state!

Radha. [*Aside.*] It's true. That is the answer. What the
lady says is right!
It's up to You Kanhaiya to relieve Me of My plight -
For heaven's sake - Your impact on us girls is too severe!
It's like a fiery Doom Volcano's exploding right here.

Paurna. [*Warmly.*] So, find a quiet place quick, child,
and start writing a letter!
Your friends will deliver it directly to Shree Krishna.
                    [*Exeunt Radha, Lalita and Vishakha.*
Paurna. [*Walking.*] Krishna's very close by, Nandi.
[*Loud lowing.*] Grand. What splendid cows!
I must see to my ablutions - opportunity allows.
                    [*Exeunt Paurnamasi and Nandimukhi.*

Vrindavan Forest.
Enter KRISHNA.

Krishna. It was sudden. I was stunned! She was
lightning – I was hit!
Familiar interests gone ... find I'm removed – more like a
hermit!

[*Looking around.*] What's My companion up to? Supposed to've fetched My spring-flower garland...

Enter MADHUMANGALA.

Madhu. Just why my comrade's in this mood be good to understand;
I'll find out in due course - I'm sure He will reveal His care.
[*Walks and spies Krishna. Aside.*] That golden-blossom tree-vine's caught His full attention there;
I'd say, the way He falters, someone's etched upon His heart,
Emblazons it decorously – no doubt, Radhika-art!
[*Approaching.*] ___Right. This is for You ...

[*Presents garland.*

Krishna. [*Oblivious.*] The goal in sight – top sacred quest:
My kewda-flower gold, lightning beauty, 'cross My cloud-dark chest!

Madhu. [*Aside.*] As I thought. ___Hello, dear friend! So, tell me what's going on?
In front of You, addressing You, I am – but You were gone!

Krishna. [*Dissimulating.*] I'm sorry friend - distraction – it's a right intriguing vine.

Madhu. Yes – something very agile, sort of strolls – that type of vine?

Krishna. Absolutely, friend, but just how does it choose direction?

Madhu. Oh, leave the humbug out, my man, if only for a second!
Be honest, why the lonely heart?

Krishna.   [*Smiling.*] My heart's without a garland!

Madhu. Yes, without a girl... and...?

Krishna.   Your cock-sure lunacy is legend!

Madhu. Your peacock-plume crown's fallen off, and You've Your garland on You!
Who's not with it? Heavens! That's Your garland I just brought You!
Anyway, rumbustious forest-amorist - it's clear -
Radhika's pretty black-bee eyes advance their awesome power!

Krishna. [*Aside.*] This sly chap guesses everything – hm - so much for My story.
__Alright - it's true, My friend. Radhika's nature - it affects Me -
Churns Me. I'm the Ganges, She's the June full moon, you see?

Madhu. You've obviously been noticing, when She's been there in person.

Krishna. I have – been through Subal I've had the chance of observation;
[*Agitated.*] She's shy, you know. Her looks sidelong. Her brows are like two dancers -
She teaches all the deer sly looks – they go to Her for answers;
The ruby lips, though - deadly - that's when Cupid gets his bow!

Madhu. Is there a chance the two of You might get together, though?

Krishna. No! I'll see Her face, like moon-rise, some way in the distance -
My friend - you can imagine, My dear mother's plaintive rants!
Carts Me off – it's home for supper – off we go, quick-smart!

Madhu. Lot of fair, good-looking gopis, friend, so, – how'd this start?
You fall for one! You've fallen for the charms of Radharani!

Krishna. Well, Radharani lacks for nothing when it comes to beauty!
Her pulchritude, especially the flowers of Her eyes,
It gives cause for contempt for things that normally you'd prize -
I mean, the moon, for instance, or a lotus flower, My friend!

Madhu. You're sold - I knew. That, after all, of late, has been the trend;
Go on – qualify the fairness. Detail further why She's great.

Krishna. A perfect question, friend, but anyone can estimate -
How fabulous She is – by but two things when in Her presence -
The emotions she engenders are exquisitely intense;
And wild deer trail Her everywhere She goes at a close distance!

Vish. [*Off-stage.*] I'm tired! Not seen Him yet there, sakhi? Where's that cowherd prince?

Krishna. A girl! And, very close by, friend, I think. Shh! Yes - d'you hear?

Enter LALITA *and* VISHAKHA.

Lal. Oh, good - Kanhaiya's, there. Let's make our way. [*Approaching Krishna.*] Good day, Kanhaiya!

Krishna. Lalita sakhi – forest-bound. You've found a leaf for writing?

Lal. Been written on. And You knew that, You've no need be pretending!
One lotus foil, for You.

> [*Places love-letter in Krishna's hand.*

Krishna.   [*Aside.*] Oh, I could not have hoped for more!
Be still My beating heart!

Madhu.   For sweets! It's that what foils are meant for!
You're writing on a sweetmeat tray, you realise, Lalita?

Krishna. Read it, friend – I'm happy if it nourishes the ear.

Madhu. You cowherdesses - you're all talk! It's priests' wives have my vote!
They're feasting everyone most days - 'bout time you chaps took note!
[*Reads letter.*] Once seeing Your fine portrait, handsome, You entered My heart;
There's no escape, and in this way, from You I never part!

Krishna. Not easy, friend, to understand the meaning of the lines.
You may have to repeat so what's communicated shines.

Madhu. Once seeing Your fine portrait, handsome, You entered My heart;
There's no escape, and in this way, from You I never part!

Krishna. [*Gratified. Aside.*] These girls are very sensitive about leading good lives -
I'll wear My moralizing hat. [*Apparently affronted.*] __Must say, it's a surprise!
You foisting lady-matters on My companion and Me -
Our job's watching our cows around the forest boundary;
You girls can't just turn up like this, and say things that might taint us!
We shall have to tell the elders – I'm afraid you shan't detain Us. [*Walks impatiently about.*]

Madhu. [*Trying not to smile.*] O brother celibate –
there's no one disciplined as You;
You've put them in their place, You stood your ground, stuck with what's true -

It's a disgrace - this carry-on's a matter for your mother!

>*[Turns Krishna to go. The girls exchange shocked looks.*

>*Krishna.* She could have come to Me, Vishakha, can't say that I know Her,

If She's fallen for some charmer, I suppose I ought to help Her.

>*Vish.* Yes! You should! You've what it takes - who in Gokool's like You?

When well-bred girls like us feel down, *You* lift our hearts - it's You!

The lifter of Gokoola's hill – well, who was that but You?

This letter, for good reason, Krishna's, been addressed to You!

>*Madhu.* Dear me, *all* of the herdsmen lifted up that hill - I saw!

They all threw up their canes, that's what - was cowherd-sticks galore,

How come you suppose that it was my best friend alone?

>*Krishna.* It's stretching it a bit, Lalita. Stick to what is known.

>*Lal.* You've kindness, then, for every single villager, but one?

Why purposely aggrieve Her, Krishna? What is it She's done?

>*Krishna.* Oh, come, now, come - slow down – would Madhumangal let that go?

Or, Shridam, even fast asleep, he's keeping Me in tow.

Besides, Mathura's king makes sure the laws are well in place;

To aggrieve a high-class girl, young thing's, a serious disgrace!

>*Lal.* [*Losing patience.*] So mean! So mean, and yet He smiles – look how He's simpering!

Humbug stories - nothing more! That's all that He loves styling!

I'm shocked that Radhika fell for this outright cowherd scoundrel!

Just a box of cheap tricks, of which we've been dealt a sample! [*Cries.*

Madhu. Charmed, I'm sure, but He's as versed in good conduct as me;

He's very tuned – in Him, bad conduct's not something you see -

And stop the beastly crying!

Vish. [*Aside.*] Well, an actor He may be;

But, Radha's berry necklace – got to touch Him inwardly;

There's no doubt whose it is__Kanhaiya - going to give You this:

It's nice. Will suit You. Extra special gunja berry necklace!

[*Offers Him the necklace.*

Krishna. [*Smiling, apparently impatient.*] Gorgeous! Oh, indeed - but tough! Too hard. Looks good - but faulty;

That's girls for you - you know! Nice chain – but, sorry. Not for Me!

[*As if oblivious, He returns His garland, instead of berry necklace.*

Vish. [*Aside.*] And so, His blunder favours us.

[*Hides it in her dress.*

Lal. True colours by degrees -

Turns out the marvellous celibate's a snake who injures gopis!

Radha's love is so misplaced, friend – we'll make sure She's through!

Vish. Well said, sakhi! [*They start walking.*

Lal. Vishakha. You know where to go to, don't you;

Be sensitive with our dear friend. Make sure She gets the garland!
I'm going to find the holy lady – let her know what's happened.

[*Exeunt Lalita and Vishakha.*

Madhu. Could have been a bit more p'lite, my friend. They're p'lite to You;
When ego's on the rise - I'll tell You – one thing's always true -
One finds oneself with vertigo, on top of Mount Remorse.

Krishna. You're right. Joking like that, sakhe. It's true. Was rash and worse.

Madhu. Gone. Not seen for dust, the feisty girls are on their way.

Krishna. [*Regretful.*] She'll probably be heart-broken. He's wicked - cruel, they'll say!
Might keep Her chin up first, sweet girl, but then She'll turn against Me;
And torment - I know what it's like. Does anyone get free?
From Cupid's provocations? I feel bad I was so boorish,
Neglect a tender shoot of love like that? For what? Just foolish!

Madhu. So what's the plan from here?

Krishna.   The plan's to write back straight away!
Except for that, I do not see that there's another way.

Madhu. Write a letter – how? With what?

Krishna.   Some ink from China roses!
It's perfume charms a heady spell, that's what the folklore says.

Madhu. That big wood full of China roses isn't far at all,
Let us press on!

[*Exeunt Krishna and Madhumangala.*

Enter VISHAKHA *and* RADHA, *en route to Sun-god temple.*
VISHAKHA *is reviving* RADHA.

Radha. And I really just don't care about what all the elders think…
You know, you're very kind – I must have pushed you to the brink;
Know any decent ladies' standards, friend, I won't ignore?
Made no difference – all of My desires get shown the door!
[*Starts to fade.*

Vish. [*Flurried.*] Alright, alright. It's alright, really. Nothing's wrong, my friend…
[*Offers Radha the garland to smell.*
Radha. [*Restored.*] Enfeebles Me, recharges Me. Stopped trying to comprehend.
Vish. [*Dressing the garland on Her.*] Don't bother. You can't analyse the way You are affected -
Why does this Krishna-garland here revive a dizzy head?
Why does His name have magic mantra-power that takes control?
Why His fine perfume has more allure than any jewel?
Radha. [*Aside.*] Kanhaiya-the-wonderful rejects Me utterly!
Don't see the point in being - hobbled state's no way to be.
Lake is what I need. It's deep and cool – don't want to suffer.
__I'd better make My way on to the Sun-god shrine, Vishakha;
Could you let Jatila know, please? As I promised I'd be there.
Vish. I'm coming too! Almost forgot I'm s'posed to go for prayer!
Best to please Jatila – very glad for the reminder.
Off we go! [*They walk.*

Radha. [*Soberly.*] Sakhi. I want the lake! I want deep water!
Prince shuns Me, I am burning badly. Only way to go.

Vish. I see lots of good omens, so we'll hear no more of woe.
Less talk, my friend! [*They reach the wood of China roses.*

Radha. [*Looks ahead.*] It's looking like an early sunset, sakhi.

Vish. It's Rose-Wood! Sunset-crimson roses - what we need precisely!
The Sun-god loves these roses - pick some! Perfect flowers to offer. [*They collect flowers.*

Re-enter KRISHNA *and* MADHUMANGALA.

Krishna. The rose's beauty, friend, was stolen from the lips of Radha.

Madhu. Marvellous. Press some. Pretty ink to do the serious writing.

Krishna. [*Taken aback. Unsteady.*] No, wait! D'you sense that glow? Same glow as Golden Meru mountain?
And that's bejeweled ankle-bells - you can't mistake the sound!
Angels in the wood! The divine goddesses around!

Madhu. That's the one we're after, sir - the victim for the trapping!

Krishna. [*Jubilant.*] You said it, friend. Behind the trees - and lets find out what's happening! [*They hide.*

Radha. [*Clasping Vishakha. In tears.*] It's when you speak of Him, sakhi, He floods My memory!

Vish. [*Tears brimming.*] You're so self-assured - how could You get this disturbed, sakhi?

Radha. It's that rascal, dear friend. My better character's been stolen;
His chest stole My discretion. Blanked it totally. It's gone!

His moon-like face shrivelled the flowers of My vows to religion;
And shyness was dismissed with, in a brutally quick fashion -
Sacrificed. On posts. The stunning posts that are His arms!
Hopeless, really, friend, because besides these awful harms,
The python of His glance, that look - it eats Me up completely!

Krishna. It's Krishna who's bamboozled, girl - He's lost to *You* completely!

Radha. [*Folding her hands.*] Why would You mislead Me so? I haven't yet grown up;
You led Me, I was wide-eyed - 'long the path You led Me up!
That led to nowhere, prince – how is it You are so detached?

Krishna. Detached? You are My life, beloved – how am I detached?

Radha. [*With a sigh.*] I'm giving you my pearls, sakhi. I'm very fond of these. [*Tries to pass Her necklace over.*

Vish. [*Firmly resisting.*] Why would You torment me, sakhi? Would You explain, please?
No - I don't want to take them - we're still waiting for Lalita! [*Cries.*

Radha. You're crying! I'm the one who's been mistreated by Shree Krishna!
I want you to arrange something for when I die, alright?
My arms tied round a tamal tree - make sure they're nice and tight;
Don't want to leave Vrindavan – ever. It's the place for Me...

Krishna. [*Tearful.*] This is the most perfect love, dear friend, you'll ever see!

Radha. [*Aside.*] Time to go. I have to. This pain's getting too much for Me.

__I shall venerate the Sun-god. Just as we were told to, sakhi;

Bathe first, of course - while I'm away, you carry on with picking.

[*Takes two or three steps. Aside.*] No more Kanhaiya?

[*Turns back.*

__Sakhi – can I ... well, there's one last thing;

Don't have your painting, do you?

Vish.   Friend – I only wish I did!

Radha. [*Despondent.*] Of course. I'll have to meditate, then. One more time beloved. [*Meditates.*

Krishna. I'm drunk on some outrageously strong liquor for the ear!

Can't help Myself. You, join me! Come, My friend – let us draw near. [*They come out from the trees.*

Vish. [*In a flurry.*] What a yogi! Goodness gracious! Look! Get Your eyes open!

[*Opening her eyes, Radha is astonished.*

Yes! You've got the trouble-making culprit peddling passion!

Peacock-feathered crown - a brand new peacock-plume edition;

The very cowherd boy responsible for Your condition!

Radha. It's a splendid dream...

Vish.   If that were so, it's something new:

Dreaming minus sleeping? No! It's real - nothing but true!

Krishna. Flower-petal glances say I'm welcome - yes, I'm sure!

How poised, My goodness Me - will stir when ready, not before;

An angel! Lotus flowers stand out, but this one? Heaven-sent!

Radha. [*Eyes surveying Krishna. Aside.*] Well done Me. That was indeed a little time well-spent...

Krishna. [*Smiling.*] Ah, cunning Vishakha. Stroke of luck that you turn up;
Searched everywhere to say how wrong it was You set Me up;
Offering Me a feeble excuse for a berry-necklace -
Purloining My prize garland with noteworthy artfulness!

Madhu. Take it, sir – just go and get it off of Radha's shoulders!

Krishna. I can't believe you said that, sakhe – what would that afford us?
I wouldn't deign to brush a woman by – not in My dreams!

Radha. [*Aside.*] He's joking. Mind, you just can't tell – dead serious, He seems.

Vish. [*Laughs.*] That's a shame when there's no pretty damsel can resist You!
But, You do manage to wear whatever gifts they give You, too.
It's Your sly look so attracts them - impressed gopis stop their blinking,
And find out more excuses to engage You – offer something -
Peacock plumes, and unguents - a nice red berry necklace?
Or any ruse they choose in their pursuit of happiness.

Krishna. [*Aside.*] Oho - a gorgeous smile! Brows raised as tight as Cupid's bow;
Black bumblebee eyes roaming, sottish - stinging like a foe!

Jat. [*Off-stage.*] Vishakha? Daughter?

Krishna.   Old Jatila? Is it ... ? How's she here?

Enter JATILA.

Jat. [*Spots Krishna. Aside.*] Kanhaiya? What? __ Vishakha – I've a mind to bend your ear!

The incense, sandal and the saffron – you forgot them!
Why?

Krishna. [*Aside.*] Chakora-bird Kanhaiya making headway in the sky,
Nearly at the the moon-rays that He drinks to stay alive;
And along comes a wretched cloud-bank - how's He to survive?
___Beloved Aunt!

Jat. Young charmer - stop Your leering at young gopis!

Madhu. [*Laughs.*] Much too harsh – my fellow friend is only proper – always!
Honest eyes. I've noticed, though - do you - have you a squint?
Need to deal with that ...

Jat.   Scarcegrace! You tell me why You're present!

Krishna. It's obvious, dear lady – all these roses - mesmerising!

Jat. [*Aside.*] Is this the meeting Lady Paurnamasi's organising?
Apparently, He's got some kind of talent she's engaging.
___I still think, though, it's time for You to leave here, Master Charming.

Krishna. Oh, look – there is no rush, old thing – don't you be anxious, there.

Jat. [*Scowling.*] My daughter-in-law's beauty - it's a fact's - beyond compare!
To find the blessed girl with You, all good sense cries 'Beware!'
You have no conscience, no restraint - send sly-looks everywhere!

Krishna. You really have Me wrong, good aunt - I don't like the critiques;

I revere your daughter deeply, all the more so when She speaks ...

Jat. This dawdling, Vishakha!

Vish.   [*Smiles.*] Being shocked's what caught me out!

[*Throwing a distracting glance.*] Disgraceful deer, dear lady – just a no-good gadabout!

Hopping grove to grove - ignores his loyal doe's true passion.

Jat. I despair with you – you have some kind of deer-obsession!

Madhu. My friend, how does that thirsty parrot shun sweet pomegranate?
Tell me.

Krishna. [*Smiles.*] Well, it's not as if the parrot doesn't want it,

He's patient in the matter of the beautiful fruit's ripeness.

                    [*Vishakha signals Radha a knowing-look.*

Radha. [*Aside.*] Phew. [*Containing herself. To Vishakha.*]
I so want to hear much more - oh, what a chance to miss!
It's rotten luck, My friend – I hardly, barely get to glimpse Him!
The awful crone – just only ever in the way - so grim!

Jat. [*Aside.*] Long's my girl's alright, Kanhaiya gets to have some credit...

__Gone midday, Vishakha – Sun-god duties to be met.
Look lively!

                    [*Exeunt Jatila, Radha and Lalita.*

Krishna.   Friend, we know where Radhika is sure to be;
Moonlight-Radharani follows new-moon Paurnamasi!

                              [*Exeunt.*

ACT III.

Rendezvous.

> *A mango grove. Late afternoon.*
> *Enter* PAURNAMASI *and* LALITA.

Paurna. I'm baffled, child. That Nanda's son's declined to meet your friend!

Lal. Perplexing prodigy, good lady - hard to comprehend.

Paurna. Look, there - in the Burflower grove. A spot of luck, young thing!
And Madhu right there too, beside the son of Gokool's king!
[*Reviewing.*] Prince Charming has His nice gold flute with all the sparkling gems;
Diamonds, sapphires. Very dainty - rubies at both ends.

> *Enter* KRISHNA and MADHUMANGALA.

Krishna. [*Regretful.*] I've a burning for a closeness that I doubt will ever be,
Was rude again – too flippant. Radha shan't be pleased with Me!
Her friend took it all lightly, but My banter was unkind.
[*Sighs.*] Madhu, friend, the soft-eyed girl's great cunning steals My mind;
[*Animated.*] Back there - Her string of pearls did not just 'snap' before She went:

Not so! For while retrieving them, in that contrived instant,
She sent a melting glance My way - with old Jatila present!

    Paurna. [*Conclusively.*] Those sighs carry on, and all
His jasmine flowers'll die;
Eyes aren't steady, either - who's done this to brave
Kanhaiya?
He's miles away. Some beauty has Him all wrapped up in
thought.
I do believe, my dear, by Radharani, he is caught!

    Krishna. [*Sees Paurnamasi and approaches.*] Namas
te, good lady!

    Paurna. Boy – dwell less on gopi-curves!

    Krishna. [*Amused.*] You didn't need to say that, and as
anyone observes,
I don't touch winsome gopis ...

    Madhu.   [*Laughs.*] We're pursuing
one, though, aren't we?

    Paurna. [*Humorously.*] Your manners are impeccable,
Krishna - You're Nanda's son;
You're brave - the village revels in heroic things You've
done;
But, lovely as You are, why madden gentle Radha so?

    Madhu. Wait, that's put the wrong way round – not
sure why you don't know:
It's Radha maddens Him, good woman – makes Him go
bizarre -
His crown, bugle and staff - all lost. He's no clue where
they are!

    Krishna. [*Embarrassed.*] The boy's absurd, it's sad,
good lady – one thing I don't do -
I don't dote on your gopis – if that's challenged, proof is
due;
Ask him, please, he knows it's so!

    Madhu.   It is, it is, good lady,

No hint, or trace of saffron that He wears was on them lately!
You do see gopi make-up on *Him* sometimes - here and there...

Krishna. [*Good-naturedly.*] Can't be trusted, can you, dolt - can't take you anywhere!

Paurna. Come, but what the lad's said's true, brave boy, they all love You -
Gifted, handsome, and inspiring, and always surprising too -
They might be at home, but if the gopis hear Your flute;
Suffice to say, the upshot is they're dress-sense-destitute!

Madhu. Oh, never mind the flute, good lady, let me tell you this -
He steals the girls' clothes personally - when they go bathing – yes!
I've seen Him in broad daylight filch them - up and round His shoulder!

Krishna. [*Frowns to check Madhumangala.*] My flute-music, perhaps, good lady, has a unique nature;
But that could not affect your patient gopis, goodness knows.

Lal. Mantras, then? Or potions? What's the way You predispose?
A cunning rogue's passed on to You the methods that You own?
How do You rob good gopis of their happy lives at home?

Madhu. I'd say you're right, Lalita - use of mantras and so on;
Seen the demons, high as hills, He's battled with and won?
Hands down, and look at Him - as cool and placid as a lotus.

Lal. Brahman boy, your good friend burns. He isn't cool to us!

Madhu. Oh – cool, but starting fires as well, friend?
There's the gopis' claim;
That's plainly sorted with a touch – just so, and …
> [*Places his hand on Krishna's chest
> and removes it quickly.*
> Hot as flame!

You're right, Lalita. Ouch! [*Reflects.*] Oh, but, Lalita, I forgot!
It's Her! Right in His heart, She is - Radhika's why He's hot!
His default's cool as moons – but not since Radha's come
along.

Lal. Kind boy, be realistic – His heart's casing's
diamond-strong;
How'd my friend gain access when She's delicate and
tender!

Madhu. My friend feels for yours in the most tender
way, you monster!
For Her, and Her alone – He never sleeps – gone all ascetic!

Krishna. [*Bashfully turns away.*] I wish that you'd
grow up. It isn't funny. Any of it...

Lal. [*Aside.*] I like how this is going for my girlfriend.

Paurna. Krishna, listen -
Seriously, no jokes – I want an answer to my question -
That river racing past the banks of household sentiments,
Past Religion Bridge, and hills of mounting moral
judgments;
It's Radharani-river rushing madly down to You!
Who reached Kanhaiya ocean, but, then what's Kanhaiya
do?
He rallies vicious currents of indifferent words – don't
argue!
Now, what's the explanation?

Madhu. He can't help it, don't you see?

It's springtime cuckoo-songs - that's what makes people lovey-dovey!
An awful din I always stop effectively - no fuss;
My bow sorts it out, lets feathered friends know who is boss...

  Paurna. Moreover, moon-faced boy, that isn't where this story ends!
In the evenings, Radharani's being held back by Her friends.
When jasmine flowers, the kind You wear, diffuse the air with scent;
The girl's dismay is palpable. Know what makes Her fallfaint?
It's camphor melting on the porch - the rising of the moon!

  Krishna. [Aside.] Serious is the word...

  Paurna.   Dear boy, beware. Don't court misfortune -
If someone shows affection for You, happily return it,
Otherwise things turn sour quick. So, don't forget - please learn it!
The sun's attracted to the east, each day arriving there,
East should be pleased and welcoming, but no - it couldn't care;
The upshot is, the whole earth's sunk in darkness black as ink!

             [Krishna bows His head.

  Paurna. [Observes him with satisfaction. Aside.] Good – He's got the picture – a compliant, right-eye-wink.
__For now, stay by the mango tree, alright, my handsome one?
A sakhi will be here before the setting of the sun;
She will know where You're to go, to settle all this squarely.

  Krishna. [Humbled.] Yes, good lady.

        [Exeunt Krishna and Madhumangala.

Paurna.   Right, Lalita - let's find Radharani!
I'm happy. [*They walk.*

A laburnum grove.
Enter RADHA *and* VISHAKHA.

Radha. Listless. I feel languid. It's that wretched smile of His;
All that sweet talk sakhi - is the hope that We'll meet pointless?
What kind of sweetness is it puts one's well-being in danger?

Vish. Ridiculous! That You can't see how You endear Kanhaiya!
Your love! That's how, but You don't even see that that's, the special!

Radha. Look, dawn's a long ways off, and Cupid's consistently baleful;
Doubtless out to dash My budding hopes before the morning light;
Fat elephant like him does that - squash flower-buds at night!
Oh, why won't things work out, sakhi?

Paurna. [*Encountering Radha.*] Lalita – ready, right?
Let's see how detached your friend is. I'll do all the talking...

Lal. As you say!

Paurna. [*Approaching Radha with apparent despondence.*] My dear? Please know that Krishna's mood's unchanging;
Your company's is what He wants, some precious moments with You;
Says You're the only answer, and it's only You will do.

Radha. [*Very moved.*] I'm going to confess! [*Folding Her hands.*] It's true - He's very, very dear -

He's the cloud that saves Me burning up in a wildfire!

Paurna. But think, Jatila's girl – consider how He came from heaven;

In which sense, what You want, you know's, a difficult ambition;

Look, don't be in a dream-world, like a child who wants the moon;

Oh, I know you'll recognise the actual situation soon.

Radha. [*Stuttering.*] If you're sure. Alright. I will - let thoughts of the prince go;

I do need one big favour, though - should have asked long ago -

I want to be a honey-bee – please bless Me now – tonight;

If I can be helped in that away – then, everything's alright.

Vish. Careful, noble lady – She's not looking very stable!

Paurna. [*Urgently.*] Astonishing, it is – poor thing is really in a muddle!

[*Holding Radha.*] Alright. It's alright, dear – my, my, You're in a funny state;

Now, hear what I'm about to say so You can get things straight!

Was going to say, my lovely, you're asleep to how things are -

Fact is, You are idolized by heaven's gods - You are!

And Krishna is possessed of such intense desire to see You,

He's looking frail because of it - it's absolutely true!

Lal. What's He play his flute for? Every song is meant for You!

Always making ornaments and bracelets to put on You!

Your names are the scents of springtime bowers to Gokool's prince;

Radha's beauty in each forest flower's to Him intense!

Radha. [*Calmer. Aside.*] Calm down, now. Think clearly, Radha. Don't start up again...

Paurna. That's wisely put, Lalita, dear. So briefly, here's the plan, then:
Vishakha will bring Krishna over from the mango grove -
Meanwhile, wait with Radha here, in this laburnum grove.
Hide her from the elder's wives, alright? I've things to do.

                    [*Exeunt Paurnamasi and Lalita.*

Vish. [*After walking some way.*] Here we are, there's Krishna waiting by the mango tree...

Re-enter KRISHNA.

Krishna. [*Expectantly, facing West.*] Well, nearly dawn already. Aye - the sun just met the sea,
And, jumbo-calming, night-owl-soothing forest-dark is in.

                    [*Watches the path.*

No sakhi? Where've they got to? [*Turns to face East.*] That's one very bright moon shining,
A lotus-closing, gopi-waking moon cascading broadly -
What girls who meet their loves in secret never like to see.
[*Perplexed.*] Radha's only problem is too much regard for dharma;
And, elders' censure, too, would, no doubt, bother and alarm Her.
Something untoward's come up – My messenger's not here!

Vish. [*Peeping out from forest cover.*] Kanhaiya's looking my way. Right, let's start looking sincere -
This is going to be fun!

Krishna. [*Encouraged.*] Vishakha sakhi! Waving too!

                    [*Approaches.*

Beauteous friend! You too are like the goddess Rambhoru!
Radhika and Vishakha – you are hard to tell apart!

[*Vishakha is subdued and remains silent.*
You're quiet. What's wrong, My friend?

Vish. I can't ... I don't ... where shall I start?
Handsome – I am so unhappy!

Krishna. [*Hesitant.*] What's all this about?

Vish. Kanhaiya, this is hard – but, You should know what I've found out.
[*Dramatically.*] It's that big fool, Abhimanyu, prince – he's going to take my friend!
To Mathura! [*Breaks off in dry tears.*

Krishna. [*Vexed.*] When exactly?

Vish. Now! It's very much this second; You were with our lady when he seized his chance to get Her...

Krishna. [*Stricken.*] Vishakha, why? What made him go?

Vish. Suspects that She's Your lover.

Krishna. Why does he suspect Her?

Vish. Why, to look at her – who wouldn't?

Krishna. Gone? That's it? That's it? How does time pass with Radha absent?
Dreadful! Droning bees buzz Cupid's ridicule of Me;
The moon is sparking angrily, the breeze tormenting Me!
[*Becomes lost.*

Vish. [*Flurried alarm.*] I ... no, no, I was joking – sorry - seriously, Kanhaiya!
She's absolutely fine – what, with the garland that you gave her!

Krishna. [*Relieved.*] Rascal! That was awful.

Vish. But, the whole idea's just nonsense!

Krishna. You say your friend shows love, sakhi? You think there's evidence?

Vish. Like when She hears Your name - She could be miles from where it's spoken -
And straight away, She'll mumble, tremble – that's what happens. Often!
Dark clouds – that's another thing. She wants to go and hug them!
Desire for wings rampaging in the lotus-eyed girl's bosom!

Krishna. Come on now, take Me to this girl who feels these marvellous things.

[*They walk.*

Re-enter RADHA *and* LALITA.

Radha. Why so long? Might be that something's diverted that sakhi;
Perhaps she couldn't get the prince to trust her properly?
Fate's just out to get me, give Me pain and misery -
Like now – it's like Shree Krishna is a hundred miles from Me!

Vish. [*Observantly.*] Safely say Your Radha rather eagerly awaits You;
Peering through the branches - trying to get the path in view;
Can't stay still at all, see that? See now She's by Lalita?
Now She's sitting down again – I bet it's tiring for Her.

Krishna. Moon-rise, stars and lotuses are all not short of charm,
But this girl's face, and gleaming nails and smiles, wholly disarm.

Radha. [*Discouraged.*] Maybe He's been distracted by another girl that loves Him -
Why not? He could quite easily decide to leave Me lonesome...
Tragic! Night like this, moonlight cascading everywhere -

No prince! It makes this forest bower seem desperately bare.

Krishna. [*Catching up with Her.*] Brightest moon - I think it's awesome – 'stonishingly clear!

Radha. [*Aside.*] I can't believe My fate! My stars! He's actually here! [*Freezes.*]

Vish. Radhika – don't freeze, girl! Now what? Something caught your tongue?
You banter with the prince – we're gopis, sakhi – oh, come on!
Don't shake!

Lal. You can't be shy, Radhika – that, I must advise;
Here's the charming prince, and it's not time for butterflies,
Confidence and strength will underwrite Your enterprise.

[*Firmly holds Radha before Krishna.*
Look at poor, dear Radha – why've you thieved Her heart, like this?
You know what You're doing, and it's not good – You're remiss!
You lure Her swan-like heart with Your enticing lotus-face;
Then stun it with the eyebrows – you should know that's a disgrace!

Krishna. [*Smiling.*] But, Lalita, I am not the type to steal from a young lady.

Vish. You're honest as the day is long, it's so - undoubtedly;
Where our clothes go after bathing, to this day's, a mystery...

Krishna. Lalita, name the way, sakhi - I'll prove My honesty!

Lal. Well, there is a test, prince, yes – and it's foolproof. Completely.

Krishna. Very good. Well, you announce what said test would entail;
I've every confidence My good repute's set to prevail.

Lal. I'm glad You're confident, perhaps You know the
pot-snake test?
'Magine Radhika's a pot-snake in the cleavage of Her
breast;
You're tasked to take the snake's crown jewel - that's
Radha's centre-piece;
If Your hand's steady, then, some of Your said repute will
cease.

Krishna. [With false alarm.] You're serious, Lalita?
Can't believe it. No, don't smile!
It's just a minor matter – why d'you need a pot-snake trial?

Radha. [Apparently indignant.] Lalita, you please stop!
[Frowns at Lalita.

Lal. Vishakha, why's Radha objecting?
I'm trying to clarify things!

Vish. Well, it's not really surprising.

Lal. I'm listening.

Vish. Her concern's for Him. A very risky test.
Besides, we know His record – do we need to make Her
stressed?
He wasn't harmed in dealing with that massive Agha snake,
Or that hydra full of hatred in the deep Kaliya lake;
The python troubling His father, He just magicked into
spirit!
Not likely that the pot-snake test's the right one for Him,
is it?

Lal. [Smiling.] I still think it would work, Radha –
especially in your case;
Yes, Krishna rides the Bird-king, and He gives great vipers
chase -
But, I believe what You have's going to sort Him out, quite
frankly.

Radha. [Apparently angry.] Alright, Lalita! Understood
– I'm here for you to mock me!

I'm going to let the elders know, and no one's going to stop Me! [*Tries to go.*

Lal. Silly – goodness sake, we have an opportunity! No speculation – thief, or not. We find out - You go after!

[*Catches hold of Her sari.*

Krishna. Alright! If you insist, I'll do the wretched test, Lalita! [*Goes up to Radha.*

Lal. [*Observing Him with scrutiny.*] No, wait a minute, there, Prince Charming – or, rather - Prince Thief!
Well, well - Your hand's already even shakier than a leaf;
Apart from that, Your goosebumps clearly give the game away;
So, certified a thief – oh, yes – a prince of them, I'd say!

Krishna. [*Meekly bows His head.*] Ingenious, you maidens. Raise my hands – I am not honest ...

Lal. Exactly so, and, well said. From Your own lips - splendid test!

Krishna. I want to change, sakhi – for how - I do need your instruction.

Lal. Best thing is, You go and find helpful association;
The sages in the mountains would be good – they're very kind;
Heed them well and You will heel your corrupt state of mind.

Krishna. I'll do it! I feel hopeful, sakhi – 'preciate you deeply!

[*Happily approaches Radha and gives Her His hand.*

Radha. [*Stuttering.*] Handsome, ... d-don't be silly.

[*Leaving Him, She disappears into the trees.*

Krishna. [*Bewildered.*] Where's your good friend now, sakhis?!

Lal & Vish. We'll find out for You, Krishna. [*They find Radha.*] We've got Him, Radharani!
Let's keep Kanhaiya on his toes – you're good at role-play, sakhi.

Radha. [*Shrewdly raises an eyebrow.*] At role play, Lalita? I do not do mean and teasing.
I do not do that kind of thing - perhaps I'd best be leaving...

Lal. [*Returning to Krishna.*] Our good friend's anxious, handsome. She's concerned She could upset you.

Krishna. Oh, come now, sakhi - My princess just tells Me what to do;
She commands – I do – that's it; there's really no more to it!

Lal. I know, I know – I'm sorry – I don't want you disappointed;
Better that you weren't asked to this night-time rendezvous;
It's awkward, prince – the last thing that I'd want say to you!
Makes me sort of nervous, hot – expect my face looks funny...

Krishna. [*Aside.*] Not sure, is she acting here? Just might be fooling me.

Radha. [*Showing Herself slightly.*] I don't want to be seen, sakhi! Tell Him - please, go away!

Krishna. [*Anxiously. Aside.*] Don't try and judge a young girl's heart - impossible to say,
I'll never understand them. ___Radhe, after all your pleas!
I must admit, it does seem odd, You run off in the trees;
I've joined You – I can't help it – I can't not come, actually;
Yet, there You stand. Keeping away. Aloof - demonstrably!

Lal. It's not Radha's fault, Kanhaiya – religion is to blame -
Bad for loving feelings – guilty conscience is it's name.

Krishna. But, religion's no place, sakhi – not where there's real, true love!
Think of Indra's wife's affair in holy-heaven above.

Lal. The case You cite's most apt - it's undeniable, young scholar.

Radha. [*Unexpectedly.*] I'll speak, Lalita. 'Fore I go – I know what's for the better.
[*Addressing Lalita.*] I have to keep the faith the senior ladies have in Me;
My family's very noble, and My husband's very wealthy;
Better Krishna's eyebrow-antics blush the cheeks of Cupid;
They're not going to provoke Me – I know that would be stupid.

Krishna. [*Studying Radha, He sighs with relief. Aside.*] Not a bad performance, but, an obvious smokescreen;
Those nervous eyes light up Her diamond pendants emerald green;
My beauty's slipped a smile that says Her friend scripted the scene.

Lal. [*Aside to Vishakha, seeing Krishna's reaction.*] Vishakha, look! He just cheered up - Her acting's not so keen.

Vish. Oh, dear!

Krishna. [*Smiling.*] Alarming ruse, Lalita. You shouldn't forget -
Can't catch a hefty elephant in a spider's tiny net!

Vish. Radhe, we've done our best - time to be nice to Your beloved.

Krishna. [*Tenderly.*] Please! My ears are ringing, precious – shocking what You said!
If You say some nice things now, I know I can recover;
I do deserve a hug – that beastly Cupid's out to torture!

Vish. Handsome should remember, Radha's modesty incarnate;

She'll need some coaxing, I suggest - maintain a cool, calm state.

    Krishna. [*Respectfully.*] I'm cool and calm - so very so, I dare say this, my friend -
Radha could drape Me round her breast – I'm cooler than a garland!

        [*Krishna begins gradually approaching Radha.*
    Radha. [*Nearing Vishakha.*] Vishakha – could you help Me, sakhi? I am *not* at ease!

    Lal. But, Radha, here to soothe you, like a cool wreath charming bees -
Is the kindly Krishna-garland. It's not Vishakha You need!

    Radha. [*Acting cross.*] Shameless! Yes, Lalita, you've gone way too far, indeed!

    Vish. Radhe – who ensures that we're all safe here in Gokoola?
Kanhaiya - makes no sense, sakhi, to distance brave Kanhaiya!

    Krishna. Pretty Radhe, it's quite simple – the truth is, you overpower Me!
I don't see how there could be any cause at all to fear Me!
Your razor-glance, Your dancing brow - for Me, the game is up!
Your falling locks see any lasting strength of Mine's washed up!
Not used to it at all, I swear – but that is what you do.

    Lal. It's really so, Kanhaiya? That she gets the better of You?
I didn't think that that was something anyone could do!

    Vish. You know that He's devoted to all those whose hearts are true -
And yours is so, so You should hold the good prince close to You!

Where's falseness get us, fair one? - false pretence will just not do...

Radha. [*Indignantly.*] D'you know, Lalita's ruined you, Vishakha, sinful thing?

Krishna. I just don't understand why Radha's so unwelcoming;
I seem to be shut out, Lalita – all deprived of kindness.

Lal. Our good friend's straightforward, see, Kanhaiya – maybe talk less?
She isn't Chandravali – not impressed with silky chit-chat.

Krishna. How will I win your friend?

Lal.   With practicality - like that;
Like we assist her.

Krishna. [*Delightedly turns to Radha.*] That, can do. Had hoped to have the chance -
Fixing flowers in braids, massaging fatigued arms, for instance;
Can draw vermilion patterns round her blouse well-skilfully. [*Krishna reaches Radha.*

Radha. [*Retreating, She affectedly points a finger.*] That's it! And I will not forget this moment, corrupt sakhi;
You've had Me in your clutches, but I'm going home - bye-bye!

Lal. [*Holding on to Her sari.*] Leave Your heart with Him, and now You're going home - but why?
Gold's spent! It's been consigned. Has truly left the purse, Radhika ...

Radha. Will you please leave my sari – I am going to tell Mukhara!

Mukha. [*Off-stage.*] Yoohoo! That you, Lalita, darling? Seen your dear friend, Radha?

Lal. Mukhara's here!

Krishna. [*Apprehensively.*] Which case, I think I'll take to forest-cover. [*Relocates a little ways off.*

Enter MUKHARA.

Mukha. [*Looking ahead she pauses. Aside.*] Remarkable
– from here looks like a deity of jewels;
But, Him alright; Kanhaiya's scent - the aroma that rules!
[*Shuffles over to Krishna.*

Krishna. Oh, my - good lady ...

Mukha. [*Interrupts – attempting to be stern.*] Lady
with the chronic rheumatism!

Krishna. All joy to you, Mukharaji!

Mukha.   And how's that supposed to be?
Your flute playing's not been curbed as yet, Kanhaiya -
where's the happy?

Krishna. My flute annoys you? Didn't know. In what
way, noble lady?

Mukha. You ask the girls! You ask them - they've
bizarre group-lunacy!
They can't be stopped, no matter what - their ear-holes get
possessed!
Each time you play – that's it – flute-mad - they run off in
the forest!

Krishna. [*Laughs.*] That's so outrageous, Mukhara!

Mukha.   But, Kanhaiya, I'm worried!
You in this bower - it's being so late.

Krishna.   You don't need to be worried!
Mukhara, Paurnamasi said for Me to come this way;
This very place - a darling fawn's about to come to play.

Mukha. And play it will tomorrow, lad – I assure You,
it will!

Krishna. Madam, though you're ram's-horn tough,
you know I love you still!
So be it. I take my leave... [*Disappears among the trees.*

Mukha.   Lalita? Kanhaiya's gone yet?

Lal. He has indeed.

Krishna. [*Aside.*] The poor old girl gets terribly upset;
Got to keep Radha from going, though – I'll take it very easy. [*Catches Radha's dress.*

Mukha. [*Looking intensely ahead.*] Lalita! That's just rude! My word! You think that I don't see!
That's Krishna tugging Radha's dress! You cannot lie to me!

[*Krishna – worried – steps back.*

Lal. [*Aside.*] Only thing to do's to try and dupe the dear old biddy!
[*Indignant.*] __Old thing – what can you see? The river bank down there's pitch-dark;
It's just a tamal tree – a golden root, and gloss-black bark!
And that's another gopi, standing by the swaying tree -
All it is, is leaves and branches catching on a sari!

Mukha. [*Aside.*] She doesn't ever lie. __My poor old nerves. Child - home for me;
I'm awfully tired, a good night's rest's what I need, probably!

[*Exit.*

Vish. Radhe – use Your dress to dry Kanhaiya's face – He's hot!

Radha. [*Frowning.*] That's your skill, Vishakha – you who've mopped His brow a lot;
Since you were very young.

Vish. Oh – now then, Radhe - You can too - To thank Him for His spring-flower garland – really up to You.

Krishna. While I do realise we only ever get what's due, I just wonder what those spring-flowers did to be that close to You?
And how, dark-eyes, You grant them what's impossible for Me?

Radha. Vishakha, friend, would you retrieve that necklace presently?
My lovely gunja necklace that you took without permission?
I don't have any need to keep this garland round Me on.

Vish. Dear boy, my friend is most displeased I took the necklace from Her.

Krishna. Let Her have them both! Radhe – one necklace for surrender. [*Approaches Her cautiously.*

Lal. [*Smiling. Half aloud.*] Kanhaiya returns the necklace Radha's desperately missed.
Can't avoid her blouse entirely ... but, the lady does insist.

[*Radha turns around and frowns.*

Vish. There, Radhe, dear friend – somehow, You now have what You wanted.

Radha. [*Biting lip.*] That's it, you vulgar girl! [*Strikes Vishakha with a flower.*

Vish. [*Amused.*] Excuse me? I did what You said!
- I asked Him for the necklace!

Krishna. Can't You throw one at me too?
At least a glance? If not a flower, a side-long glance will do!

Lal. Already you're amenable - why not a teeny glance?
Come - who gifts a jewel, and keeps the jewel box? That's nonsense.

Radha. Lalita, not a good idea to dice with blasphemy!

Vish. You've no need to be tetchy, sakhi – You have Paurnamasi:
The professor of trouble-shooting's absolute commitment!

Lal. [*Gratified. Aside.*] A glance of love. At last! Our dear friend's star's in the ascendant;
Kanhaiya seized by smiling eyes.

Vish. Tonight's the night, alright!
Krishna in His forest under shimmering moonlight;

Our dear friend beside Him - what a scintillating nightfall;
Her fixed, and intense adoration, fair one, crowns it all.

Lal. Oh, now I remember – all our offerings, Vishakha!
The moonstones - they'll have melted - going to spoil the
Sun-god's alter!
Quickly! Come - we'd better pick more flowers from this
meadow.

Krishna. You're incorrigible, dearest! [*Holding Her sari.*

Radha.   But, leave go! You must leave go!
My friends are calling Me!

Krishna.   Not true! Stop being fickle with Me!

Radha. [*Smiling.*] I warn You, that the Truth goddess
will vouch I'm truthful, shortly!

Krishna. [*Mildly smiling.*] Turmoil. Fairest - ever since
bewitched by Your sweet love;
Bewildered like a bee, I've buzzed around – down - up
above -
Dying for the lotus-fragrant nectar that spellbinds Me;
Possessed - I long to share Your pearls' divine locality,
With any luck, I shall be rich in pure felicity!
You know I've distanced friends, My love, they're being
absent suits Me -
The way Your pearls adorn Your bosom's caused this
languor in Me...

                    [*Radha is embarrassed.*

Oh – listen now, beloved. Ah! A sacred ceremony!
Welcomed by in-canting geese, the moon's arrived on high:
Appointed there to cool Us, have the river shine like sky;
Florescent springtime wonders mesmerize and amplify!
And there's a roof-house feeling to these homely bowers
We're by.
Come – let Us explore them!

                    [*Exeunt.*

ACT IV.

Flute Theft.

Vrindavan South – near Govardhan Hill. Afternoon.
Enter NANDIMUKHI.

Nandi. This afternoon, I'm told, Kanhaiya left for Govardhan -
Lalita saw Him speeding off – He doesn't go there often;
Soon as He got back, she says, and returned cows to pen;
Was off again – the obvious question's, what's one make of that, then?
Anyway, she's making sure His heart won't forget Radha;
To wit, master Subal's her man – now, where is he, I wonder? [*Walks.*
Here's Padma. What's she wanting?

Enter PADMA.

Padma.   Nandi, friend, I'm at a loss!
Chandravali's troubled, and I thought you might advise us?
You'd know what to say to her.
    Nandi.   So, why is she upset?
    Padma. The situation, sakhi – why's it not been addressed yet?
Kanhaiya - always in Gokool. Each day, and every evening;
You know that, of course – I'm sure for some, it's very pleasing.

Nandi. Oh, that.

Padma. Kanhaiya's rarely in our bit of the cow-kingdom.

Nandi. So happens, there's no need to fret, girl – pretty sure He's come;
Saw Shaivya's nicely made-up; forest flowers in Shyama's hair;
Bhadra's a gunja berry necklace - best I've seen her wear.
I suspect the gopis' favourite is indeed in Govardhan.

[*Flute music.*

Vrin. [*Off-stage.*] If all the world's tunes chose a tune –
that tune would be the one!
King Nanda's son's a new muse in the realm of Govardhan.

Nandi. That, then, solves the problem Chandravali's brooding on.
So, Padma, I must leave you now to catch up with Subal.

[*Exit.*

Padma. [*Looking ahead.*] That Vrinda! That enchantress, is all too predictable;
I know what she's up to, trying to worry Chandravali.

Vrin. [*Off-stage.*] So, you really want to end up as as disturbed as Radharani!
Your grandmother Karala says, it's not safe – don't go out;
I agree - I tell you, Krishna'll steal your heart - no doubt!
All the pretty Gokool-girls have lost their hearts to Him;
Side-looks from His lotus-eyes was all it took to steal them.

Enter CHANDRAVALI.

Chandra. [*Looks frantically about.*] Vrinda, fibbing? No, can't be - but, I don't see Kanhaiya!

Padma. [*Nearing.*] Are you alright, there, sakhi? I don't spot a forest fire...

Hey, watch the lips! Calm down – breathe gently –
ShreeKrishna is here;
That not echoes of the peacocks on the hillside? He's right near!
He's just outside your village, friend - He's at the forest rim.

    Chandra. [*Looks towards hill.*] Where's he, sakhi Padma? [*Embraces Padma.*] It is Him!

    Padma.   Of course, it's Him.

Enter KRISHNA and SUBAL.

    Krishna. Sunset. Ah. Much cooler, now. A welcome dusk - you know?

    Sub. My friend, Your mind's been elsewhere for a while, I know *that's* so.

    Krishna. The peacock-dancing sakhe, made me yearn for Chandravali.

    Sub. Peacock-dancing?

    Krishna.   Yes, it was that fan of its that got Me.
So many shimmering rainbow-moons, all on display before Me;
Chandravali-effect – indeed, her name means, 'set of moons.'

    Sub. There's no draw as effective as Your mellifluous tunes.

                    [*Krishna raises flute to His lips.*

    Chandra. [*Turning abruptly.*] Awesome as the time that I first heard the airborne honey!
Wicked flute.

    Krishna.   Subal, good friend – you've won Me Chandravali!

    Sub. You're welcome.

    Padma.   Go - the flute just said, make haste to Gokool's prince!

Chandra. [*Reflecting.*] My, you've got the luck, flute –
short and knotty – makes no sense.
You're dry, gappy and wooden, friend, yet you get Krishna's
kiss -
He never lets you go – good kind of karma to possess!

Krishna. [*Looks on happily.*] My eyes have become
lotuses that only flower at night;
Chandravali, sakhe's, my lotus-flowering moonlight.

[*Approaching courteously.*
Altogether gorgeous - pretty face, nails, pendants – brow;
Breath-taking as a crowd of moons – your name suits you
– and how!

[*Chandravali blushes.*
I'm fed up constraining demons, wasting time not seeing
you -
Dear girl, I really mean it - no more night-vigils - I'm
through!

Chandra. I'm surprised You're here, I know how bees
like nice fresh flowers;
I've wilted - left alone for no one knows how many hours.

Krishna. Chandravali doesn't wilt, oh, no - she's fresh,
and dewy new;
Missed you badly - nothing but a cool embrace will do!

Padma. Say a little more, then – how d'you miss my
friend, exactly?

Sub. But, it's true, the boy does really miss His
Chandravali;
Parched as a Chakora-bird who can't get to a rain-cloud!

Krishna. That's literally parched - a troubling state
that love's endowed;
In the middle of the woods, racked by the dire effect of
ardour;
Lucky there's the resource of refreshing, cooling Radha ...
[*Flustered.*] Water ... water!

Chandra. [*Jealously.*] Oh, good gracious – better be with Radha!

Krishna. Well, I said 'water', sweetheart.

Chandra. Oh, I see. So, you said 'water'? And then, another word came out? Well, well – so, how d'You do it?

Krishna. I think you may've misheard, my love.

Chandra. [*Lowering her head, hot with anger.*] I'm grateful - please, don't doubt it ...
You're always very kind – I shall recall fondly for years -
The perfect decoration ever given to two ears!

Krishna. Glad you like those gold earrings I gave you, blossom-girl,
But, I don't think I'm quite with you – a little lost, My pearl.

Padma. Don't bother with it, sakhi – chin up – it is what it is -
Obsessed with Radha, Radha's name's invading His sentences.

Chandra. [*Sighs.*] You're right, Padma, good friend.

Krishna. Right? Now I'm more confused, My lovely!
No question - Radha's certainly intriguing and uncanny:
By which I mean Radha-the-star that's miles from planet earth!

Padma. I imagine that that star-sign's ruling You for all its worth.

Krishna. [*To Padma.*] My dear - weasel words will only worsen Chandravali -
Look how she's downcast the way that you're portraying Me!
I'm saying how I feel sincerely, not capriciously!

Chandra.[*Pretending to be calm.*] Prince, You light up Gokool life – satisfy everybody;
For You, I'd need be very dim, to not make an allowance;

Promise You, there is no problem – complaint, or defiance.
  Krishna. [*Aside.*] Formidable – concealing fury in this
dulcet manner.
__Blossom – please, it's no good if you're cynical and
bitter;
Be angry – be direct – that I appreciate, you see.
  Chandra. Can't face You, Kanhaiya. I regret being so
nasty;
Best be going home.
  Krishna. Beloved, please. Please, have a heart!
                                        [*Folds His hands.*
  Chandra. Master, why won't You believe I'm sorry, on
my part?
That's why I'm going now to pray to Durga for forgiveness.
                      [*Exeunt Chandravali and Padma.*
  Krishna. My Chandravali-moonlight, friend – obscured
by evil darkness;
What am I supposed to do? The lights gone out!
  Sub.   Oh, don't!
Comically fickle – can't see that, young man?
  Krishna.   I can't!
You can't assume too much about someone profound as
she is;
Her eyes are so sincere, you know - she sort of talks in
prayers;
So courteous, sakhe – don't think she could be angry with
Me;
Can't let the darling go - she's just so decent, Chandravali.
Let's head for the keshara groves, and come up with a plan.
                      [*They come across keshara tree groves.*
Fine keshara trees. Fine arbours - ponds abound, My man!
It it not a pleasant place? Don't you agree? No? Rather!
  Sub. [*Aside.*] Aha! [*Taking 'no rather' as 'no Radha'.*]

____No Radha? Pleasant place for
You without Your Radha?

Krishna. [Embraces Subal.] Impossible! You're right.
You're unequivocally right!
Radhika has to come here to this keshar wood, tonight!
Please tell Lalita, fellow friend!

Sub.   Sakhe - as you command us.

                                      [Exit.

Enter MADHU *and* PADMA.

Madhu. Alright then, Padma – you say He was gentle,
not discourteous?
Nonetheless, Chandravali's still angry at My friend?

Padma. That's right.

Madhu.   I'm sure, together, it's not
something we can't mend;
Boy's bound to be upset – it's time for reconciliation.

Padma. I'm with you, sir!

Madhu.   *[Looks ahead.]* And there's my friend. Poor
chap in isolation...
With no one but the bees. I cannot quite hear what He's
saying.

Padma. Let's get behind that bush, then, sir. We
mustn't miss a thing!

                                  [They hide.

Krishna. [Missing Radha.] Easy task for Cupid to
ensure infatuation;
The girl's a jewel – the fairest, rarest, divine apparition!

Madhu. There you go – He's clearly mad about your
good friend, Padma;
Let's get her - sort this out.

Padma.   Oh, that is music to the ears, sir!
So passionate about her!

Krishna.   Her allure's just heavenly!
Feel sorry for the moon goddess - not even half as pretty...
Madhu. We've got the picture, Padma!
Padma.   Let us fetch the fair-of-face!
                    [*They move quickly out of hearing range.*
Krishna. If only gorgeous Radha'd deign to share but
one embrace!

Padma. One thing, brahmana boy's, that my dear
friend is proud and wary -
To know Kanhaiya's asking for her, though, would make it
easy.

Madhu. Good point. [*Returning to Krishna.*
                    I overheard ... that moved me very
deeply, friend;
Let Your heart speak loud and clear, I always recommend;
Your dear beloved needs to know.

Krishna. [*Embraces Madhumangala.*] Then, tell Her!
Thank you, sakhe!

                    [*Exeunt Padma and Madhumangala.*
What's that? My sweetheart's foot-bells? Oh, I see – it's
only bees.
On edge with just the slightest, faintest rustling of leaves;
There's love for you!

Enter CHANDRAVALI, MADHU *and* PADMA.

Chandra.   This grove? These keshara trees,
Padma sakhi?

Padma. That's right – go on. [*They continue.*
                    [*Sound of ankle bells.*
Krishna.   The blessed bees again.
They're getting to Me!
What happens when you crave something - desire
confounds the brain.

                                                    [*Gets anxious.*
I'm more keen than a thirsty cuckoo near a cloud of rain!
                                          [*Listening carefully.*
Does really sound like foot-bells ... [*Turning in the sound's direction.*] But it is! Indeed - She's here!
[*Crossing to Chandravali.*] I'm losing wits for Radha! Precious – finally - You're here ...!
                        [*Chandravali gives Madhumangala a fierce look.*
   Madhu. [*Taking 'Radha' as 'ardour'.*] Losing wits for ardour. [*Sighs.*] Does so love you, Chandravali!
   Krishna. [*Maintaining composure. Aside.*] Chandravali? Lucky thing this boy's handy with word-juggl'ry!
__Chandravali returns because she's still a soft spot for Me.
                     [*Chandravali shyly places a jewelled garland
                                                  on Krishna.*
I've Chakora birds for eyes, my treasured transcendental beauty!
[*Exuberantly.*] While one moon captivates a hundred such birds in the skies;
I enjoy a host of moons with my Chakora eyes!
   Madhu. [*Self-satisfied. Aside.*] I know You're smart, but don't dismiss the skill just needed then,
No way You'd have appeased the girl without my acumen.
   Krishna. In Cupid's regime, friend, seems like you head up peace *and* war.
   Padma. Come, young sir – we've jasmine flowers to pick, shall we withdraw?
                          [*Exeunt Madhumangala and Padma.*
   Krishna. [*Aside.*] Radha's going to be here any second, can't stay on!
Need make a rapid exit. __Sweetheart – let's go over yon;
The groves of nager keshars – royally romantic spot.
                        [*Exeunt Krishna and Chandravali.*

The keshara tree grove. Later.
Enter RADHA *and* LALITA.

Radha. It's dark, sakhi!

Lal. I know. Well chosen finery You've got;
Not bright – it won't give us away.

Radha. That's true.

Lal. [*Surveying Her, smiles.*] Imaginative;
A sapphire necklace in Your braids – there's novelty - impressive;
Your flower-crown is slipping down, but nonetheless – still splendid;
But eye-shadow on arms and musk round eyes is absent-minded!
Can't be helped, I s'pose, when there's a scramble for the prince.

Radha. So funny. Where's the keshar grove? Well? Which way is it hence?

Lal. My dear, we are on route. [*Walks a little, has a second thought.*] Of course, it's trickier for You, though;
Other chaste young girls might cross this forest incognito - Dressed as You, demurely, on their way to see the prince - But, Your body has a lustre that betrays You, in a sense!

Radha. I will thank you to stop joking. Look. We're here now – there - you see?
Keshara trees! [*Hurries towards keshara grove.*] No perfume, though. We'd smell His fragrance, sakhi;
His nails gleam like a set of moons – but they aren't in the wood-let;
So - fun, at our expense? Suspect the prince is in the thicket.

Lal. Bur-flower tree grove opposite – perhaps He's in there, sakhi?

Radha. [*Looking there.*] You might think that You can hide from Me, but I'll detect You swiftly. [*Searching thoroughly.*
Very swiftly!

Lal. Come on, sakhi, aren't you going to help me? Doing up the hideaway.

Radha. I don't think you need Me.
Arch of flowers for a door - custom'ry lotus-seat;
A cup of nectar by it, would be nice – refreshing treat;
Let Krishna appreciate your skilfulness, young lady.

Lal. [*Sets about her tasks.*] Oh, sakhi - come on in!
Come inside and stop the worry;
Kanhaiya's been held up, that's all.

Radha. [*Anxiously crossing to Lalita.*] I'm fairly sure who by;
Padma's always hogging Krishna for her friend, that's why;
Hasn't reached the grove. Well, well. Forgotten about us;
And now it's getting lighter – rising moon is treacherous;
Foe of any girl who wants to rendezvous discretely.

[*Exeunt Radha and Lalita.*

A nager keshara tree grove.
Re-enter KRISHNA.

Krishna. Dawn already - Northern Star has vanished practically;
Lilies all deprived of bees, owls back to nests to rest.
[*Walking.*] Don't doubt this night has left Radhika thoroughly distressed.
[*Ponders.*] Must get some nager keshar flowers, it might give Me a chance.

[*Selects nager kesharas, keeping them in a pouch. Continues.*

Probably the last straw, though – can hear her losing patience:

'Where's Krishna? Sakhi – He just does whatever's opportune!'

[*Reaches keshara grove.*

[*Despondent.*] Was right – discarded camphor ... betel – Radha's sapphires - strewn!

Flower-crown in shreds! This grove narrates the entire story -

Latest disappointment made Her awfully unhappy.

[*Continues on.*

Here's where Radha worships. Sure to come sooner or later.

[*Crosses to Sun-god shrine.*

Re-enter RADHA, LALITA and VISHAKHA.

Radha. [*Sees Krishna.*] Lalita sakhi – by the shrine – untrustworthy sweet-talker.

Lal. Keep still. Don't move, sakhi!

Krishna.　　　　　My love's Her confidantes with Her; This'll take some acting. [*Approaching.*] Well. Well done -Brava, Lalita!

You had Me there! Must say, you dispense humbug with conviction!

Had Me pace a keshar-grove for hours, taught Me a lesson!

Lal. [*Hotly.*] You what? You never came! Just nonsense - You didn't turn up!

My friend lay in Her keshar grove until the sun came up! Counting seconds - night snail-pacing - waiting's got a limit!

Krishna. [*Brazenly.*] Outrageous! [*Revealing pouch of flowers.*] I've a pouch of nager keshar flowers to prove it! See – witnesses! I'm pitied - fact, the nectar they drop's tears!

Lal. So that's your game – of course – a double meaning, it appears -
You say 'keshar', meaning 'nager keshar' – that is very clever!

Krishna. You're the one who's trying to be clever, Lalita!
Juggling words, besides, I mean, [*Confessionally.*] I take the blame, I s'pose...
Me being too familiar with fair damsels, goodness knows.

Vish. So, what's wrong with fair damsels, then? Be frank – it is allowed.

Krishna. What's wrong is they're like lightning to the helpful Krishna-cloud;
Fickle, fleeting – and, yes – should have known that, as a rain-cloud.

Vish. We are not like lightning bolts! We're soft – not hard and noisy.

Lal. [*Pointing at a bee.*] Who's lightning-like, Vishakha?
[*Tunefully.*] The capricious bumble-bee!
Zipping off - the difference is, the bee is black in colour.

Krishna. [*Smiling.*] Poetic. That was smartly put!

Lal.   [*Aside to Vishakha.*] Could not have said it better;
Quite right to make the point.

Krishna.   And, I would add - what isn't true's,
When damsels take offence, they are unreasonable with you;
They state their case in such a way's to not discourage you.

Lal. [*Aside to Radha.*] He *did* endure an awkward time
– and lenience might be due.

Radha. [*Sidelong look.*] It's not that I don't know the way you fool the unsuspecting.

Krishna. [*Uplifted.*] These keshar flowers were for
Your hair – well, that's what I was hoping;

Not in vain, I trust? [*Opens flower-pouch.*] Their fragrance is on me too, treasure;
My – what a scent they have!

    Radha. [*False smile.*] Might be Chandravali's aroma…

    Krishna. You joke with Me, my treasure, but, I think, You speak Your mind;
You really think this aroma is Chandravali's kind?

    Radha. [*Smiling.*] May I have My flowers, please?
                              [*Holds out the corner of Her sari.*

    Krishna.   [*Transfixed. Aside.*] Sweet! How Her eyebrows dance!

    Vish. [*Aside to Lalita.*] Krishna's hypnotised, Lalita – in a Radha-trance!
She's got the flowers *and* flute – oh, look! Swept tidily away!
He's not the faintest clue!

    Lal.   It's Her eyes have Him in Her sway;
She's pinched Krishna's precious flute – from right under His nose!
Normally not possible, He's always on His toes -
Cowherd boys can't get it off Him, even if He's sleeping.

    Radha. [*Aside to Lalita and Vishakha.*] What distracts the lot of us from good, wholesome house-keeping?
What drags us from our spouse at night, and leaves us all dishevelled?
That architect of infamy - the flute! Herewith withheld!
To save all fair Gokoola girls, I have the cad in prison!

    Madhu. [*Off-stage.*] Hello, there, Rangini - have you seen my dear companion?

    Krishna. [*Still captivated.*] What's Madhu doing now?

Re-enter MADHUMANGALA, *holding a flower garland.*

    Madhu.   Aha! Was tipped off by Subal,

Radha's staying up all night, he says - and that's no doddle!
Said which grove. Thought I'd drop by, and, you know - say,
hello. [*Approaches*
The prince! What's happened, Radha? Did *You* hypnotise
Him so?
Gone inert. Looks lifeless. Gone and made Him petrified!
Garbed in armlets, flowers, and dyes, looks truly deified.

> [*Radha smiles.*

Krishna. My friend knows all about the rotten night I
endured, precious.

Radha. I imagine that it was, sir. Just how did you
cope? Please, tell us!

Madhu. You're sceptical – and rightly so, sakhi. Out
here is scary.
But, now, my dear friend's with You, You have no need to
be chary.
Just say the word! He'll take You home, and then - at last –
some rest.

Radha. Well, what's decided how you see me, sir -
tired and distressed -
Relates to a glowing set of moons - a Chandravali;
Krishna's moon-glow nails, you know, weren't there - I was
unhappy;
I languished in My grove all night, until the sun came up.

Madhu. [*Aside.*] She knows? Does Radha know 'bout
Chandravali turning up?
Don't think for a moment, She chose that word accidentally.
There's no point in contrivance, best resort to flattery.
___Poor prince thought Your handsomeness might not be
of avail,
But luckily, He'd recourse, so His spirits did not fail:
Chandravali was ...

> [*Krishna frowns at him - concerned*
> *looks all round.*

[*Aside.*] Sense my popularity declining...

Krishna. [*Clarifying.*] The tender lad can't disconnect
– he feels My suffering;
Remembering My nightmare last night, My friend can't go
on!
[*Smiles.*] The words I know he would have said – they're
not hard to imagine:
'Chandravali – a set of silver moons' lovely reflections;
Reminded Me of You, and saved Me from My deep
dejections!'

Madhu. Great minds think alike – it's what I would
have said exactly!

Lal. Radhe, just think clearly, and observe Him
studiously;
The clever prince bears curious tell-tale signs about His
person.
Alas, bodice necklines of fair girls is what He dotes on,
As a sapphire-clad deceiver, He's unworthy of your heart;
Deviating honest women is His customary art;
Sadly, once they're abandoned – oh-so casually -
All they've left's the shameful stain of impropriety!

Radha. It's hurtful. Very hurtful. I'm most cynically
misled!

Krishna. No, love – it's silly thinking!

Radha.   [*Reproachful.*] I know why
Your eyes are red -
You had to keep them open wide to find Me in the darkness;
Pollen from keshara flowers is why they're in distress;
The chilly night-time breeze is clearly why My master's
lip's sore;
Things happen – don't be worried – isn't You I have it in for.

Krishna. I'm very, very worried - I depend on You, My
angel!

Radha. You don't depend on anyone – that anyone can tell.

Krishna. Depend on ever-lasting You – same in each incarnation;
At any time, or lifetime, My state's lost infatuation;
Shackled by mesmeric eyes, fair bosom, waist and lips;
For Your face more fair than any - fascination never slips,
Why'd I not accept Your scolding and the marvel of Your ire?

Radha. Hear that, Lalita sakhi?

Lal.   You have famed past-lives, Kanhaiya -
But, less happy traits of some of those have filtered through:
Like restlessness and harshness. And like, saying things untrue;
Being cruel, ferocious, ruinous - intoxicated too;
Also, sacrilegiosity and murder, in my view!

Krishna. [*Smiles.*] Lalita's all extreme, My friend – Radha's unsatisfied;
And Vishakha is less likely still, to want to take My side.
                [*Takes garland from Madhumangala, bows.*
[*Sweetly.*] These, for You – near fresh as You, aroma near as fine;
Celestial garland, Radhe, for a bosom as divine!
                [*With an amicable look, He gives
                        Vishakha the garland.*

Vish. [*Presenting the garland.*] He only brings Vrindavan peace and love – it's true, though, right?
Oh come - you cannot bear the blessed prince to leave Your sight!
Young lady – with His attitude so conciliatory,
I can't understand how You can still be fey and pouty.

Radha. [*Indignant.*] Ever think before you speak?
Krishna.   I shall now happily bow down -

The one You *do* have feelings for with dust upon His crown;
He only wants one thing – a little softness in those eyes!
    Lal. Radhe! Watch out, behind! Hear? It is her - the old
girl's cries!

[Radha turns.

Enter MUKHARA.

    Mukha. Here He is, the schemer - and He has You in
His forest;
Snatched from where You're truly loved – beguiled out of
the nest;
My innocent, good child in the dire clutches of a scoundrel!
    Madhu. [*to Krishna.*] Hollow as an old flute, friend. Let
us wish her farewell.
    Krishna. The flute? The flute, sakhe!
    Madhu.   The flute? You don't know
where it is?
    Krishna. Radhika must have stolen it – is She full of
surprises -
No way I'm going without it!
    Madhu.   [*In jest.*] What? Look - so far You've
been lucky -
These girls here would steal your soul, get going! Don't
you see?
Forget the blessed flute, sir, come – we'll make a run for it!
    Krishna. [*Smiling.*] Moment, pretty friend. [*Crossing to
Radha.*] Must say, You do deserve some credit;
A brilliant skill there, fair one – So, You've commandeered
my flute?
    Radha. [*Black-browed.*] How dare – how very dare
You! What would I want with Your flute?
Who knows where the wretched thing is?
    Lal.   We gopis don't thieve -

We're decent - You're so brazen it's a hard thing to believe!

Krishna. Lalita sakhi, as a friend, please be straightforward with Me.

Lal. I am - we've talked enough, and now we're going home directly;
Far's Your dreaded flute's concerned, we don't care, and don't know!

Radha. [*Shifting to Mukhara's side*] This is what He's like – keeps on discrediting Me so;
Asserting I'm a thief, good lady!

Mukha.   Radha – please don't worry...
[*Furious.*] Slanderer, Kanhaiya – so You know, You don't fool me!

Madhu. That's not fair, old thing – She's using you to back the fibbing;
This girl of yours did pinch the flute!

Krishna.   There is just no denying -
Mukhara – My friend's being truthful.

Mukha.   Answer him, Radhika.

Radha. Good lady, we'd not relocate a stick from this wood - ever:
Not even for a sacrifice!

Krishna.   [*Smiling.*] You didn't take the flute, then?
So what's with the dancing eyes, flushed cheeks, light-hearted grin?

Mukha. [*Raised voice.*] You're talking to the wife of Your own uncle - Abhimanyu!
I can't believe my ears – that sort of talk does not become You!

Madhu. Mukhara, I promise - swear it on the holy lore!
My friend just paid respects to Radha - head to floor - I saw!

Mukha. [*Gratified.*] Did He? May be hope for Him, then.
                         [*Smiles all round.*

Nonetheless, Kanhaiya -
Sheer dalliance, as You should know, won't please Your father, Nanda,
You've cows – go and take care of them.

Krishna. Without My flute, good lady?
How will I control the cows? Without it, it's not easy.

Lal. Your concern's controlling girls – say what You mean, Kanhaiya.

Krishna. Very bold with the good lady here, I'm noticing, Lalita;
No point in Me protesting ...

Mukha. [*Enraged.*] This is just downright improper!
Behaving in this way towards my modest, shy granddaughter!
And me! An infirm lady, who can barely find her way!
So, You should just go home, prince – home. And, I mean straight away!
Otherwise I'm going to take this matter to the king!

Madhu. [*Furious.*] You tell Mathura's king, then – we don't care, old, feeble thing!

Mukha. [*Bluffing.*] I'm going! Come granddaughter! To the chambers of Mathura!

[*Exeunt Mukhara, Radha, Lalita and Vishakha.*

Krishna. Sakhe – You and I need get My cows down to the water.
[*Walks, turns, sighs.*] One moment calm and patient, next unreasonable and skittish;
Stand-offish, then expressive of a tender, heart-felt wish;
Artless gaze, preceding cunning side-wise look of ardour;
Rancorous, then loving, no? So goes divided Radha!

[*Exeunt.*

ACT V.

Radharani Relents.

In, and around Gokoola Village.
Enter PAURNAMASI.

Paurna. There's trouble in affairs of love, it's just the
way it is;
Radhika's situation is beset by serious worries. [*Sees
arrivals.*
Who's here with Madhumangal? [*Recognising.*] Why - the
forest creatures' sovereign!
Vrinda, the enchantress - wonder what she's here for, then?

Enter VRINDA *and* MADHUMANGALA.

Vrin & Madhu. Greeting to you, mother!
Paurna. Bless you, dears!
Vrin.   Why, noble lady -
Why are you upset?
Paurna. Because, child, Abhimanyu's angry;
He knows Radha adores Gokoola's precocious young
master;
It's dismal! Abhimanyu wants to leave here for Mathura -
That awful, spiteful mother of his, menacing poor Radha.

Vrin. Paurnamasi has the antidote to any dismal
matter.

Madhu. Why have you such sympathy for Radha, noble lady?

Paurna. There really is no reason, dear, it just comes naturally.

Vrin. For love, you'll never really find a rational explanation,
Why's the star Canopus get a Wagtail's full devotion?

Madhu. Please say a little more - what is love's character, pray tell?

Paurna. In many ways mysterious. Illogical, as well;
A loved-one never likes to hear praise from the one they love,
But, criticism's something that they can't get enough of;
The bond exists outside the realm of any vice or virtue.

Madhu. Radha and Kanhaiya's love is trending that way too.

Paurna. My dear, there never was a more intensely loving couple;
Love, with Radhika and Krishna, is entirely transcendental!

Vrin. Have you noted, noble lady – now - that Krishna's spirit's low?
No bugle or staff with Him – it's not like Him, you know.
No flute melody-making from down by the river-shore;
He's not Himself – not even wearing kunkum any more.

Paurna. How so?

Madhu.   Chatty Lalita's how.

Paurna.   Lalita? S'pose could be.
Been helping Radha wind up in a mood of jealousy?

Vrin. Appears she has.

Paurna.   Where is she, now? Where did Lalita go?

Vrin. Subal will know - he went to look a little while ago.

Enter SUBAL.

Sub. Good day, dear lady!
Paurna.   Subal – where's Radha and everyone?
Sub. Mukhara's place - the mango tree outside - that's where they've gone.
Paurna. Alright, so, Madhu dear, I'll head off there to catch Radhika;
Let Krishna know I've gone - might help to make His dark mood brighter.

                    [*Exit Madhumangala, with a smile.*
Vrin. [*To Subal.*] Take this note for Radha, Subal – hand it to Vishakha.
Sub. Will do.
Paurna.   I'll clarify things – Radha's sure to lighten up;
We'll be back to happy groves soon as we're over this hiccup!

                    [*Exeunt Vrinda and Subal.*
[*Walking.*] Where're you going, Lalita?

Enter LALITA.

Lal.   Oh - to see you, noble lady.
Paurna. Everything alright?
Lal.   Good lady, things are out of order!
My dear friend gets tricked by that repeat-offender bounder;
And straight away forgives the scoundrel – what am I to do?
Paurna. She was let down, but it is something of a tangled issue;
In fact, it wasn't Krishna's fault - it's Madhu who's to blame;
Impetuous at times.
Lal.   [*Aside.*] Yes, Nandimukhi said the same.

__Radhika's there, dear lady – that's Her, by the mango tree;
She's rambling away now. Look. You see! How jittery?

Enter RADHA, *talking to Herself.*

Radha. Sweet talk will get You nowhere – yes, I did discard Your garland!
Enjoyed hearing complaints directed at You by My friend!
Did not ask You to bow to Me – I did not ask for that!
Ooh – it made My heart a burning cinder's habitat!

Paurna. Closer, girl - quite something, this intensity of passion -
Shhh! [*Drawing close, unobserved.*

Radha. [*Generally vacillating.*] But still, He is a sight for any girl to feast their eyes on...
[*Perturbed.*] Lalita's going to call Me harebrained – so unfair on Me!
[*Passionate.*] I can't help want to hold the handsome cowherd close to Me!
[*Frustrated.*] What tiresome, useless deity invented jealousy?

Lal. [*Aside.*] Kanhaiya is the problem, girl – *I'm* not Your adversary!

Radha. [*A bee catches Her attention.*] Ah - an emiss'ry of Krishna – you've, a message, humble bee?
An invite – oh, I see – yes? Well, He's phrased it very nicely.

Paurna. [*Wryly.*] Now, if you're really jealous, insects speak to you, you see?

Radha. [*Astonished.*] What? He's here! I'm telling You - won't let Kanhaya embrace Me!

Paurna. This love with Her's creative – fantasizing Krishna's there!

Radha. [*With an utterance of displeasure, She turns.*]
You're certainly a cheat, sir – don't persist – please, go elsewhere!
Chandravali's devotee's not going to make a fool of Me!

> [*Impetuously throws down a flower
> from her ear.*

You may've forgot - the forest trees can vouch You're dastardly!
Presuming on the innocent befits You, does it, master?

Paurna. Radha's passion's taking off – go to Her - quick, Lalita!

Lal. [*Crossing to Radha.*] I'm sure I heard some chat, Radha? But, no one here but You...

Radha. [*Interrupted. Aside.*] How's that? I am alone! So, where's Kanhaiya disappeared to?
[*Anxiously.*] __Kanhaiya was here, it seemed so - not sure how He does it;
Telepathy, I think, but it was much appreciated;
More peaceful, Lalita. Seems My rancour has abated.

Enter VISHAKHA.

Vish. Got a message from Subal, sakhi – he just now handed me it!

Lal. [*Takes note and reads.*] My dear, the jasmine flower, that's prized so highly by the bee;
Must take care not to knock or daze the creature accidentally;
In case, rebuffed, he finds another flower that makes him happy.

Radha. [*Dejected.*] I'm trouble! Awful, really, friend - prince rightly's fed up with Me;
A bee *would* shun an arid, prickly flower with acrid pollen!

> [*Is despondent.*

Paurna. [*Aside.*] As likely as the moon renouncing moonshine.

Vish. It won't happen!
I knew You would be like this, friend, and now you'll have the answer -
Nandi's just returned from finding out about Kanhaiya ...

Enter NANDIMUKHI.

Nandi. Why are You so rough with Him! To be so harsh! With Krishna?
You're soft! Since when are You harder than butter in a larder?

Radha. How is Kanhaiya, sakhi? How's He keeping? Is He happy?

Nandi. He does have one resort – He takes to dreaming of You, sakhi;
Mostly, the prince is dour, though – not one orchid in His hair.

Radha. [*Embracing Vishakha.*] Vishakha - Radha's dreadful - bless the prince that He'd still care;
Can't tell you just how much you girls have been a help to Me!

Vrin. [*Off-stage.*] Flute out of Krishna's hand – my forest deer have gotten lucky!
No interrupted grazing; as for cuckoo serenades -
No more interrupted singing! Also, good for cowherd maids -
For once they will be home on time, without their ways waylaid!

Radha. [*Reveals flute.*] The prince's flute is nat'rally bamboo of highest grade;
How are you so naughty - casting spells on honest gopis?
No way to behave, friend.

Vish.   Plays a tune, faced in the breeze;

Turn the flute, that's it, sakhi – it is extraordinary.
　　Radha. Let's see. Like so, My friend? [*Does so.*
　　Vish.　　　　　　That's it – oho - that's really lovely!
Mind - don't want Kanhaiya's friends to hear!

Re-enter VRINDA.

　　Vrin. [*Joins Paurnamasi – who's out of sight.*] Hear
that, good lady?
Music - very indiscreet!
　　Paurna.　　　　　　My, dear – you're telling me!
That's what you call bad timing!

Enter JATILA.

　　Jat.　　　　　　That Kanhaiya's here – I know it!
Was on the flute – was Him! [*Astonished.*] Good lord -
what's this? Radhika has it!
Radhika with Kanhaiya's flute, and by my stars, I'll get it!
One way or another - my big chance, and I will take it!
Softly, softly. [*Swiftly vengeful.*] Reckless gopi - flute, please!
Don't you dare! [*Pulls it away and holds it tight.*

　　Lal. [*Aside.*] Bad idea – the biddy nabs the flute -
comes out of nowhere!
　　Jat. Exhibit A for Paurnamasi – this time she'll believe
me!
　　Paurna. Vrinda, dear – this isn't good – she's heading
for my place, see?
　　Vrin. I've got this, don't you worry - not a problem,
noble lady!
　　　　　　　　　　　　　　　　　[*Exit.*
　　Lal. [*Nervously, behind Jatila.*] Isn't how you think,
good lady - please do listen to me!
Found it by the river – didn't think we should just leave it!

Jat. You think I was born yesterday, you addle-headed nitwit!

Re-enter SUBAL.

Sub. Jatila – oh, dear lady – there's a raid upon your house!
That feral monkey, mad for butter – robbing you, the louse!
Jat. [*Turns round.*] You're right, Subal - she is! I'm robbed! The greedy wretch! My butter!

[*Exit. Dashing off.*

Paurna. Kakhati the old monkey. My, my, glory be to Vrinda ...
Sub. Ooh. Jatila got her – flute hurled like a javelin, Nandi!
Paurna. Grab that flute, Kakhati! Shift that flute right up that bur tree! [*Delight all round.*

Re-enter JATILA.

Jat. I didn't think, Subal – the flute - I threw it. Gone and lost it!
But, child, to save this sister of yours, we must now retrieve it!
Sub. One big monkey, that, good lady ... em ... respects your cousin -
Cousin Vishal, he can help – he's somewhere round the mountain.

[*Exit Jatila.*

Paurna. Phew, the old girl's out the way - well done, young master - first-rate!
You didn't miss Lalita's nod – stepped right up to the plate.
Lal. [*With a sly look.*] Come, Radha, friend – the flute is ours!
Radha. [*Aside.*] Now that was really lucky ...

Enter MUKHARA, *sweeping aside stage curtain.*

Mukha. There you are, Vishakha! Abhimanyu's notified me:
Best day for Durga worship – all th'astrologers agree!
Bring Radha and the off'rings to the altar by the fig tree!
    Radha. [*Aside to Lalita .*] This isn't fair!

                    [*Looks up at Lalita.*
    Lal.   That Abhimanyu - who's he think he is?
Better get the offerings - calls for service-time are his.
       [*Exeunt Mukhara, Lalita, Vishakha and Radha.*
    Paurna. [*Proceeds uneasily with Subal.*] It's not going too well, dear, nonetheless, we've things to do -
Let's perk Krishna's spirits up – your job - and Vrinda's too;
I'll tell the ladies' council that Jatila's going barmy -
My job, that.

                             [*Exit.*
    Sub. [*Sets out.*] Here's Vrinda waiting at the tamal tree -
Ah – and she's retrieved the flute!

Re-enter VRINDA.

    Vrin.   Subal – no need to tell me.
    Sub. Least we have the flute, let's go!
               [*Proceeding, they reach Krishna.*
               Kanhaiy looks awfully love-sick.
I don't think Madhu's helping, Vrinda. What'll do the trick?
Little unprepared - what's the best means to bring Him round?
    Vrin. Not a happy prince beside that ball tree, I'll be bound;

Isn't – is He, Subal?

Sub. That is what I'm saying, Vrinda - What's the best approach, then?

Vrin. [*Deliberates.*] I think ... ah! I've got the answer!
Yes - that'll cheer Him up – we need disguises, master Subal;
Yes, indeed - let's do it!

[*Exeunt Vrinda and Madhumangala.*

Beside a ball tree.
Enter KRISHNA.

Krishna. [*Languishing.*] I'm obsessed. And, not a little;
It's Radha North, it's Radha South, it's Radha West and East;
Above, below - from Radhika there is just no release!

Madhu. If Paurnamasi's with Her now, dear friend – and so she is -
You'll be with Radha very soon – you won't be waiting ages.

Krishna. It's true – if She were satisfied, I'm sure She'd hurry here -
With Lalita by the hand; announce Herself when near -
That jingle-jangle bracelet-chiming stands the hair on end!

Madhu. Well, as it happens – that there *is* her bangle-chimes, my friend!

Vrin. [*Off-stage, in Radha's voice.*] That's Him, Lalita sakhi! Can you see Him by the ball tree?
[*In Lalita's voice.*] Yes, but mind the bees – they sting – hold on! Wait, Radha sakhi!

Madhu. [*Pertly.*] Hey - what's wrong with You, dear friend? It's Radha and Lalita!

Krishna. [*Keen.*] She's here – the one who gives my eyes such bliss.

Madhu. [*Proudly.*] You seem surprised, sir;
I am a go-between of keen resourcefulness and skill.

Krishna. What holds them up, sakhe? The girls. Mean - why're they waiting, still?

Madhu. It's alright – Radha's jolly, look – that's very clearly so;
Your flute tucked in Her sari's proof enough – that's how you know.

Krishna. That girl's beauty's never short of simply overwhelming!
Moon's lasts for a little – but, by morning will start fading;
A lotus flower's beauty lasts, but, then it's gone by evening.
[*Avidly approaches.*

Vrin. [*Off-stage, left, in Lalita's voice.*] Radiant Radha's apprehension, I'm afraid, is not abating!
After all, Kanhaiya's still involved with Chandravali.

Madhu. Lalita – radiant Radha's who He loves, obviously..!

Sar. [*Off-stage, right.*] Oh, Kanhaiya! Message for You!

Madhu. [*Suspiciously.*] Who's this?
Vishal's sister?
It is. Sarangi – look!

Krishna. I know – don't worry about her.
No, no. It's fine.

Enter SARANGI.

Sar. Was told to come and let you know, Kanhaiya -
Mukhara's annoyed you've been maligning her granddaughter;
Kakhati has the flute, she swears she's seen the monkey with it.

Just saying. Anyway, at least You now know where to find it.

Krishna. It happens that my flute's being returned to Me, Sarangi;
But, thank Mukhara for Me.

Vrin. [*Off-stage, in Radha's voice.*] Back. Stay out of sight, sakhi!

Sar. [*Objecting, facing off-stage, left.*] Radhe? Abhimanyu said to worship at the fig tree;
Why're you here?

Vrin. [*Off-stage, in Lalita's voice.*] Hala Sarangi - you can go and whistle!
No different from Jatila, monkey-face - time you got real.

Sar. [*Angrily.*] You're horrible, you wicked thing! Lalita - you know what?
I'm telling Aunt Jatila - now!

[Exit.

Madhu.　　　[*Dismissive.*] She' s Bluffing. Safe forgot. Nice young sprite.

Vrin. [*Off-stage, in Lalita's voice.*] Get rid of it! Just dump it, Radha sakhi!

Madhu. Catch that? What Lalita said?

Vrin.　　　[*Off-stage, in Lalita's voice.*] Thieves girls' of decency;
Chuck that pipe away! The thief who robs our clothes can have it!
The two go well together since they share the thieving habit.

Krishna. [*Smiling.*] She's got it in her hand now, sakhe – think she's going to throw it!
Go! Go, pick it up!

[Madhumangala does so.

Jat. [*Off-stage – distant.*] Ye gads - Sarangi wasn't bluffing!

Krishna. [*Uneasy.*] Oh, no! The mean old buzzard,
sakhe – this direction flying!

Madhu. Oops – she does not sound happy – doesn't
look that friendly either!
Not brandishing that cane for laughs, old merciless Jatila!

Jat. [*Off-stage.*] Disgrace, you are - conniving every
day! What's to be done!?

Madhu. Got Radha quaking!

Vrin. [*Off-stage, in Radha's voice.*] What, good lady?
I've done nothing wrong!

Madhu. Biddy's got 'em! Radha and Lalita. That's
them gone.

Krishna. [*Anguished.*] What's Jatila going to do? She's
mean - not nice, that one;
You stay with them, friend – you keep your eyes on them,
alright?

[*Exit Madhumangala.*

[*Sighs.*] If, indeed, My wonderful liaisons comes to light;
Abhimanyu will react at once – and does he have a temper;
Could well lock Radha up, or even take Her to Mathura!

[*After a few moments, He hears
uproarious laughter.*

Re-enter MADHUMANGALA.

Madhu. Well! That was amazing, friend – Radhika's
got some magic!

Krishna. Magic? How?

Madhu.   Was plain to see – before your eyes
- in public!
Jatila has Radhika up before the ladies' meeting -
Oof, she's harsh, Jatila ...

Krishna.   Go on.

Madhu.   Hard to watch - distressing -

But, soon's Radhika's veil gets raised in front of all the women -
It's Subal underneath, sporting a very winsome grin!
    Krishna. [*Smiles.*] And then?
    Madhu. The laughing stops, they turn on old shame-faced Jatila,
Who tears off quick as lightening!
    Krishna. And Lalita ... ?
    Madhu. Looks like Vrinda!
Radha did a mantra on her – 'markable conversion!
    Krishna. Yes, not Radha's magic - though, I see what's going on;
It's Vrinda-entertainment. Yes - a commendable show!
Since Abhimanyu holds things up, I'm gratified she did so.
    Madhu. [*Laughing.*] Was Vrinda! 'Course it was! As they went in Mukhara's house -
I saw Vrinda showing Subal how to put on Radha's blouse!
    Parrot. [*Off-stage*] You should see poor Radha - how Her Krishna-love torments Her;
Making Her friends miserable to see the torture drain Her!
    Krishna. That means a lot to me, dear parrot! Does indeed, sakhe.
    Madhu. Vrinda's parrots parrot anything she has them say.
    Krishna. I want to see our Vrinda-Subal duo, straight away!
Ready, friend?

                    [Madhumangala gives Krishna the flute, they walk.

My long-lost flute – I've missed the chance to play.

                    [Plays flute.

    Madhu. [*Listens attentively.*] Luring all the sparrows, 'tirely captivating hearing -

Irresistible vibration - 'dorning like a divine earring -
Such earrings be the makings of the flute's enchanting
voice!
[*Second thought*] Hold on - real earrings chiming in – my,
my - *two* sounds of choice!

Enter RADHA and LALITA.

Radha. I guess you can't be blamed, flute, after all –
you're just bamboo;
Still, it's deleterious – all the music that you issue!
You're being piped in nectar, why d'you pipe out bitter
poison?

Lal. Kanhaiya's fluting by the ball tree, sakhi!

Madhu.   [*Observes with a smile.*] Halt the mission!
[*Facing Krishna.*] Our objective's turned up, friend – behold
Vrinda and Subal!

Krishna. [*Warmly.*] The very two! Sakhis! Of sakhis,
oh, the best of all! [*Crosses to them.*]
Bravo!

Radha. [*Smiles. Aside to Lalita.*] Lalita sakhi - your
friend really thinks I'm Subal!

Krishna. Uncanny – look, sakhe! Now that's called
skill, Madhumangal -
As if Radha and her confidant were there in front of us!

Lal. Our cowherd's pleased to see us, Radhe.

Madhu.   [*Impatient.*] Yes, alright,
mendacious!
No need, Vrinda - it's Subal, no need to call him Radha!

Krishna. Not at all, sakhe! I love it! I love hearing
'Radha'!
I also like to say it too: [*Next to them.*] O Radha - please,
embrace Me!
Sweetheart - 'til now that heaven's been consistently
denied Me.

Lal. [*Stands in front of Radha.*] Yes, that's very funny, but we know You know it's Subal!

Madhu. [*Angry.*] You're exactly like Lalita, Vrinda – just plain anti-social!
Let Him have a laugh ...

Re-enter VRINDA.

Vrin.   Embrace the boy under the tree!
Not a problem, Radha sakhi.

Madhu.   [*Astonished.*] Vrinda – stay your sorcery!
It's completely futile, my friend here won't be phased by it!

Vrin. It is the treasured girl, I do assure you, my dear pundit!

Krishna. [*Astonished.*] You mean, this one with the garland is the one beloved Radha?

Madhu. Sorry, Vrinda - I'm confused – tell me a little slower -
Radha's at the fig tree, no? She's at the Durga-puja?

Vrin. Her counterfeit has taken over duties with Vishakha;
Her double - you'll remember, sir – had no such splendid garland.

Krishna. [*To Radha.*] Looking for some scraps of glass, and did we score a diamond!
Subal's act did sparkle, but, you can't be copied, precious.

Radha. So, now You know who's who ... and yet You stand so close to Us.

Lal. Yes, my Radha is unsettled for the sake of Her pure love;
You, lucky Kanhaiya've no intense feelings to speak of!

Krishna. I tell You, Radha – You've the beauty of the starry sky!
Oh, everything about You – not a soul who could deny -

Your lips, Your words, Your jewels, Your joyful radiance -
contagious!
Shame You vow repeatedly, to never once embrace Us;
It truly devastates – the distant, couldn't-care-less air!

 Vrin. Yes, are You not worn out, sitting up there on
Your high-chair?
He's downright devoted – what's the sense in silly fuming?
Be softer with Your forest-consort - He finds it frustrating!

 Krishna. Hard or soft, Radhika - I rely on You to be!
Just like a Chakora-bird has moonlight-dependency.

 Radha. And, You'd confuse a wizard, even! [*Cries.*
 Lal.   I said it's what happens;
You fall in love with Nanda's son, the crying never ends;
But, You won't take me seriously - all I get's scowly
frowning;
It always happens, girl – it's no surprise You find You're
crying!

     [*Krishna wipes away Radha's tears.*
 Radha. So, why aren't You ashamed, duping an
innocent, like Me?

 Krishna. It's true that other gopis do distract
occasionally;
But You're no less than supernatural wonder for My eyes;
That something in each season draws a bee's no big
surprise;
But spring's what captivates him - spring's the season for
the bee.

 Vrin. That's the truth, what Krishna says, sakhi.

 Krishna.   Please, stay with Me;
The forest's Our's, and I just want Your company,
sweetheart.

 Vrin. The forest's Yours, sakhi: [*Looks about her.*]
Spring flowers - my masterwork – my art!

Come jasmine, let me see you out! Kamalas – join the play!
You - golden yuthis – don't be shy! Lavangas on display!
Lotus flowers - let's have you! Entertain Krishna and Radha!

Madhu. She's got a way, young Vrinda. Just a few words – and, ta-da!
Flowers erupt!

Krishna.	The flower-fragrance - marvellous, sakhe!

Madhu. You like any flower, friend - there's one that's up my driveway -
The golden yuthi – Your Ma wears them while she's making ghee.

Lal. [*Smiles.*] You're expert on most anything, sir – even botony!

Madhu. [*Impatient.*] Take kimshuka-flowers, friend – ugly - crooked - like the gopis!

Lal. Vrinda, I'd say cowherd boys are same as scentless roses;
Looking good, but functionally, altogether useless!

Madhu. [*Angry.*] You gopis are by nature folk who do away with niceness!
Like how you churn your milk and subtract all the goodness-ghee out!

Vrin. [*Smiles.*] Don't forget, Lalita, who it is you're calling out;
They've ropes and sticks, and lurk in woods, and don't abide the law.

Krishna. [*Smiles.*] You're biased, Vrinda – siding with them, but I know the score;
The gopis bribe you off with all those milk sweets you adore.

Parrot. [*Off-stage.*] Gopis have a crooked nature - that is true about them;

By contrast, Prince Shree Krishna models 'greeable decorum -
Always civil, charming as a breath of springtime breeze!

  Krishna. Why, thank you, cock-parrot!
  Madhu.   What a scholar, if you please -
You'll go far, feathered-fellow!
  Lal.   Do you mean, that low-class pest, there?
Hope a night-hawk eats it!
  Krishna.   He deserves his favourite fruit-fare -
Get pomegranate seed, sakhe!
  Madhu.   Why not Lalita's teeth, sir?
I think, as a reward, it's possible he'd like them better.
  Maina Bird. [*Off-stage.*] But, the prince's love, sadly,
lasts less than sunset's red;
Radha's love's consistent, ever-flowing, undivided!
  Lal. [*Gratified.*] That Maina bird deserves a prize - for
striking parrots dumb!
Bless you, friend!
  Krishna. [*Aside.*] These birds can talk – our Vrinda's
trained them some!
  Madhu. Hey there, scurvy prattler – I don't like your
beak – catch this!

       [*Throws his staff to scare away Maina Bird.*

  Radha. They've flown! Who knew that birds could
speak with such poeticness?
  Krishna. [*To Radha.*] O gentle girl, these vines,
seducing bees with honey-drips,
Are home to any number of bright wild-life fellowships;
And all this is beguiling, but the moment You're before me;
Does' eyes aren't as lovely, jasmine climbers aren't as
pretty!
A cuckoo's song seems dull and flat, when You begin
conversing;

A peacock's no distraction from Your gorgeous locks there, flowing!

    Vrin. But, the river's lotus-lilies, I would say, are as divine -
They stand out against the water, with a Radha-divine shine!

                    [Vrinda picks two lotus flowers.
    Krishna. Though, even so, they worship Radha - that's the idea, there:
To celebrate Your smiling face, that is so very fair -
Lotus-lilies, as in worship, move in circles on the breeze.

    Vrin. [*Gives lilies to Krishna.*] A red one, and a white one, Krishna. Autumn specialities!
Red lotus on the ear, I think.

    Krishna. [*Receives them, smiles.*] Ideal for Radha, Vrinda,
A red lotus will suit Her! [*Puts the red lotus on Radha', intrigued.*] Oh, just look in My white flower!
Another bee!

    Vrin.   Kanhaiya gets a lotus, and a bee;
'Course he'd still be there - for nectar - he's not in a hurry.

    Krishna. I bet he'll go for red as well – the red lotus is pretty;
What'd I say? Look, there he goes – on Radha's red one, see!

[*Radha tries to shoo the bee buzzing around her. Krishna's amused.*]

Whirling bracelets – watch out, all! Take care – She's looking frantic!
Don't know if you can oust a bee if it's a nectar-holic,
Looking too intent on that there flower on Radha's ear, though!

    Radha. [*Fending off with her sari.*] The beastly bee won't go!

Krishna. Sweetheart – stop threatening it so!
No point waving Your sari – let him have his nectar, precious!

Madhu. I've no time for bees, friend – pesky bees don't land on ... us! [*Strikes the bee with his staff.*

Radha. [*Applauding.*] Thank you. I'm very grateful, sir!

Madhu. [*Looking around Her for the bee.*] Can I, eh ... ah – gone!

     [*Radha hears, 'Can I, eh', as, 'Kanhaiya'.*
That was fast – he's vanished!

Radha. [*Becomes lost.*] He ... I see. Kanhaiya - gone?
Forest fire, I suspect. Did I ... did I upset Him?
That's the way He is - these rendezvouses - you see, He has them;
All abrupt. Unfair, though. Shouldn't leave Me in the forest!

    [*Krishna lets others know not to intervene.*
Was going to string more flowers for Him to dress around His chest;
I have His in My hair. I know - I've thrown flowers at the prince -
No harm meant, but when He goes – things start to not make sense;
Forest closing in, and dark. All suddenly unfriendly...

Vrin. [*Aside.*] Certainly not making sense. Her love. Makes Her not see!

Radha. [*Alarmed.*] Turns a harmless throng of bees into a deadly cobra!
Sets trees on fire – no autumn blooms – it's flames on the ashoka!
Kimshuka buds are Cupid's arrows aiming right for Me!

       [*Loses composure.*

Krishna. [*Takes Radha's hand.*] Precious - what's come over You? You're everything to Me!

You, whose beauty's past compare - whose love's past comprehending.

Radha. [*Composed, but bashful. Aside.*] That's really alarming - couldn't tell what I was seeing!

Krishna. Why's the pomegranate quake? It's not the breeze – we must concede;
Your bright lips mock its flowers, Your teeth outshine it's dainty seed,
Your bosom so defeats it's pride, the lovely fruit's knock-kneed!

Vrin. Radhe – check inside the flower you're wearing on Your ear.

Radha. My yellow flower? That's where you were - you nectar-profiteer!

Krishna. Ah, the Lord of nectar's on his golden flower throne.

Radha. Too many bees – look over there – the jasmine's gone full-blown;
Makes a bee too rowdy, so much nectar and sweet scent!

Krishna. Yes, makes a bee too rowdy, so much nectar and sweet scent!

Vrin. Radhe – there's a golden bud – now's that look strange to You?

Krishna. Weaponised by Cupid? Never know what he gets up to.

Madhu. No Cupid artifice, my friend – the handle of a cane!

Enter JATILA.

Jat. Humph, scandalous priest! Ah, good - still there – I left my cane.

Radha. [*To Lalita.*] Let's go – you ready, sakhi? This old crone bedevils Me!

[*Exeunt Radha, Vrinda and Lalita.*

Krishna. [*Aside.*] I know She'd rather stay with Me –
ah, well - not meant to be;
Old Jatila-the-tiger's spooked Radha-the-thirsty-deer!

Madhu. All yours, you old conniver – have your cane!

Jat.　　　　　[*Getting her cane.*] Subal, my dear?
Are you not tired of trying to fool me? Acting like a woman?

Krishna. [*Aside.*] You keep thinking it's Subal. [*Smiles.*]
__I promise one thing's certain:
Jatila – that's Radhika! Guarantee it's not Subal!

Jat. What is it, rascal, makes You think I need Your
help to tell?
I'm done with all Your mischief!

　　　　　　　　　　　　　　　　[*Exit.*

Krishna.　　　　　Time that we went back as well;
Let's head on back to Gokool, friend ...

　　　　　　　　　　　　　　　　[*Exeunt.*

ACT VI.

Autumn.

    Gokoola Village, near Jatila's house. Morning.
          Enter JATILA.

    Jat. [*Heading for her house.*] So, my daughter-in-law's home, wearing a yellow scarf, no less...
We'll soon find out - I'm almost there ... [*Looks ahead.*] Vishakha snoring? Bless ...
Right across my doorway, eh? Well, not for long! [*Gets nearer and shouts.*] Vishakha!
Three hours you've been sleeping!

          Enter VISHAKHA.

    Vish.   [*Aside.*] Maybe that surprises her;
The Rasa Dance went on all night – not had a wink of sleep!
[*Struggling to keep awake.*]__Temple duties, noble lady – night-time one we had to keep;
Paurnamasi fixed it.
    Jat. [*Aside.*] Is that so? Don't trust a thing;
My daughter-in-law's bed deserted, so it was, last evening.
__Vishakha – call my daughter-in-law!
    Vish.   Radhe? Friend? You coming?

          Enter RADHA.

Radha. [*Yawns, rubs eyes.*] Can't stay awake, Vishakha.

[*Alarmed. Aside.*] No - the old biddy's been spying!

    Jat. [*Sees Radha's yellow scarf. Aside.*] And so, it's true - a yellow scarf!

    Radha. [*Aside to Vishakha.*] The old girl came last night,

She saw the bank-side get-together - Sarangi was right!

    Vish. Yes, but when she came, we moaned we weren't sure where You were;

We meant it - Vrinda'd told us that You'd vanished with Kanhaiya.

    Radha. Why's she standing glaring at me?

    Jat.   [*Furious.*] What a joke, Vishakha! Eyesight problems, maybe?

    Vish. [*Aside to Radha.*] What You wearing, crazy reveller!

    Radha. Oh, no - help Me sakhi!

    Vish.   [*To Jatila.*] Oh, the scarf, you mean, good lady?

Spraying yellow dye around's the done thing in Diwali;

Really yellow now, I know – they do go overboard!

Don't be cross with gentle Radha.

    Jat.   So you know – She's not your ward!

[*Relenting.*]This married girl can't go around with frivolous young ladies;

So, please do not encourage it – no ifs, or buts, or maybes -

My son's home-life's is jeopardised, Vishakha!

    Vish.   That's unfair!

Saying Diwali is bad - in truth we all let down our hair;

Young and old alike – the entire village does, good lady!

    Jat. Does carry some away, it's true, my dear – the making merry;

Saw those girls enjoying themselves last night by the river.

                     [*Vishakha glances at Radha.*

[*Piteously.*] Vishakha, can you help me? Will you please do me a favour?

 Vish. Oh, really, now, good lady – you don't need to ask that way.

 Jat. But I trust you, Vishakha – my girl must not go astray!
Kanhaiya's not to spoil Her.

 Vish.   That won't happen - don't you worry!
Lalita's far too shrewd – she's very capable, good lady.

 Jat. Erm, where's Lalita now?

 Vish.   Why, here she is, and look - here's Padma!

 Jat. Good. Must go - I'm cowpat-drying.

              [*Exit.*

     Enter LALITA *and* PADMA.

 Lal.   Where've you come from, Padma?

 Padma. I was with Kanhaiya, friend.

 Lal.   Ah, yes, where was Kanhaiya?

 Padma. The Jasmine groves.

 Lal.   Ah cha.

 Padma.   Was Him and Madhumangala.

 Lal. [*Smiles.*] You made something for Him?

 Padma.   [*Smiling.*] Yes, I did – most certainly;
Had a jasmine flower-crown. [*Remembering.*

       Oh - Kanhaiya says to me:
My Padma gives me jasmine crowns, Lalita - fiery-dyes;
And then, He wrote this note.

     [*Gives Lalita a message written on a leaf.*

 Lal.   [*Takes it. Aside.*] Don't give Kanhaiya fiery-
dyes.
What's He saying? [*Reads message.*

     Blossom - those fine dyes of yours
are vibrant;

Bring them to the hillside! Signed, your much obliged
dependent.
[*Ponders. Aside.*] I've to bring Him Radha. Easy. Clearly to
that end.
___I'll do so, sakhi! You touch base with Radha for a second.
    Padma. [*Crosses jovially to Radha.*] Good what You
have done - it is about time, Radha sakhi;
Prince steals our clothes, You steal His yellow scarf – it
works out nicely!
    Lal. [*Smiles.*] That scarf's Hers – might seem not, but
Her scarf got doused in saffron.
Agreed?
    Padma. [*Smiles.*] I'm sorry Radhe – I'm still young. I
should get on -
Got some songs about Kanhaiya, Chandravali wants to
hear.
    Vish. [*Smiles.*] It's good Kanhaiya-songs afford
Chandravali some cheer;
Useful when one cannot see Him, Padma – good idea.
    Padma. You could sing them too, Vishakha.
    Vish.   Best not to, I fear. I wish I could.
    Padma. Why can't you, friend?
    Vish.   To Radhika, young lady?
Kanhaiya's name alone transports the girl to ecstasy!
    Padma. [*Aside.*] Always making out how her friend's
love is so fantastic.
___All very well for you, Vishakha – we're hard-pressed –
gets frantic!
    Lal. I know you've problems, Padma – but, I say –
don't be dismayed.
    Padma. So many rendezvouses – so many garlands to
be made;
There's Chandravali's braids, her lip gloss, dresses – it's a
list!

Vish. [*Laughs.*] That's hard, Padma – for us, one issue
we've got does persist.

Padma. What's that, friend?

Vish.   We know no one can really claim Kanhaiya;
Yet, we desperately want to, see? It's torture by desire!
Deluded – same's to imagine you might ever grab a star.

Lal. [*Smiles.*] Vishakha – there are two problems.
There's two issues, there are!

Vish. Remind me, then, Lalita.

Lal.   Being short on lac? Lac-making?
To rub on Radha's feet – it's worth a mention, since you're
sharing.

Vish. [*Laughs.*] Lalita, we don't need red lac, it's dyes
we need – I've said!
Kanhaiya likes dyes from Radha's feet, not lac, upon His
head!

Radha. [*Embarrassed.*] Beyond a joke - don't listen -
arrant scoundrels, Padma sakhi;
Better that you hurry to your good friend, Chandravali!

Padma. 'Deed, my good friend's waiting.

                                              [*Exit.*

Lal.   [*Aside.*] And, Kanhaiya's waiting, too!
__Radhe – Sun-god wants his tributes, we shall need a
flower or two!

Radha. [*Aside.*] With any luck, she looks to
commandeer me to Kanhaiya.
__Of course, as you desire, dear friend.

                    [*Exeunt Radha, Lalita and Vishakha.*

Vrindavan Forest, near Govardhan Hill.
Enter KRISHNA *and* MADHUMANGALA.

Krishna.   Vrindavan – never finer!
Vine flowers and floret-clusters fascinating bumble bees;

Peacock-fans exploding - river-bank up, by degrees.
[*Gratified.*] Autumn is a ravishing assembly of sound;
Teeming life - just look at that fine bull! Well, I'll be bound!
There's horns to ensure triumph in the contest for a cow!

    Madhu. I see the forest's packed with yellow
amaranths right now;
Your yellow garb's inspired a trend, Kanhaiya – nice one
too.

    Krishna. [*Aside.*] Should get my wish, long as Lalita
understood my clue.
There's no denying Vrindavan is looking very grand;
But, in Radhika's absence, even autumn glory's bland!
Time to play the flute, My trusty messager of choice.
[*Plays flute.*] I'll make it clear in any way I can - in any voice:
My angel, lovely friend – I have been waiting far too long
here,
Frustrated in the limbo of vague hope that You'll appear!

    Madhu. And what's the new song for, my friend?
    Krishna.   Entice a doe, sakhe.
    Madhu. Ah - clarify that for me?
    Krishna.   Well, she's doe-like, anyway.
    Lal. [*Off-stage.*] Music forcing forest flowers to
blossom out of season;
And milk-cows, willy-nilly, empty udders in elation;
Brook of milk - look - streaming through the forest of
Vrindavan!

    Krishna. [*Detracting attention.*] Oh, here he is, friend!
On your right - now this bull is the one!
He's called Padmagandha – got the copper horns and neck
bell;
Ruddy hooves, pink eyes – look at that awesome tail, as
well;

What d'you say? A hump like that? This snow white bull's
the best one!

Re-enter RADHA, LALITA *and* VISHAKHA.

Radha. [*Aside.*] The music came from here - it did –
I'm sure. Oh, yes – no question.

Lal. [*Pert smile.*] Radhe, those stand-up ears of Yours
are sharp as any deer.

Radha. Oh, kettle-pot, Lalita – you're the flute-
addicted deer!
I saw how you reacted.

Lal.   Radhe - who's your best-est friend?
It's Rangini, the deer – one's always like one's special
friend.

Radha. [*Aside.*] Most helpful - His perfume is a dead
give-away. [*Acts casual.*

Vish.   [*Smiling.*] Hey, Radhe!
That fragrance has You homing like a bee on a bouquet.

Radha. Vishakha – I am here for lotus flowers for the
Sun-god.

Lal. Oh, look how You've lit up – You must adore that
shining god!
The one shines in the forest, 'course - not that one in the
sky.

Radha.[*Apparently angry.*] I've a passion for the lotus
– what d'you childishly imply?

Lal. Can't keep a straight face, sakhi.

Vish.   Not behaving like a friend;
Territorial, Lalita – she's so jealous - to the end!

Radha. [*Frowns.*] You're annoying – and, you know, your
lips do not need to burn dry -
Satisfy your shabby wish – the chance is right nearby!

Lal. Radha, we were brought up in a strict and proper
fashion;

Everybody knows - so I'm surprised at what You've spoken.

Radha. [*Laughs.*] Well, one could tell this morning you're the emblem of a lady;

Kanhaiya's feathers on your arm, I think confirmed it - maybe?

Oh, yes – and then, that feather-crown, out on Vishakha's chair.

Lal. [*Smiles.*] Ridiculous assertions!

Vish. Yes - a quite absurd affair -

And You can't hide the way You feel, Radhe – you won't get far;

A moonstone on the moon dissolves, no? Things are as things are.

Radha. [*Surprised.*] Lalita, hope you will forgive me, but it's time for Me to go. [*Trembles.*

Lal. [*Puzzled.*] What's the problem, Radhe?

Radha. [*Black-browed.*] Right - as if you didn't know; Stop pretending! There He is – to think - you would consign me,

To a callous opportunist!

Lal. [*Aside.*] Opportunist tamal tree? A little like Kanhaiya from here. ___No, no, don't go – do stay!

Arranged this chance – come on! [*Keeps hold of Radha.*

Radha. Vishakha – help Me get away!

Vish. You're too in love - stop fancying Kanhaiya's everywhere!

That's not Your sweetheart - that's a tree with glossy black bark, there!

Krishna. My fair girl's not responded – better raise another tune. [*Does so.*

More keen than a Chakora-bird who's got to see the moon...

Vish. [*Faltering.*] Hold tight, there Radhe - easy! Bur-flower tree will keep You steady!

Lal. Thank you, flute, your silky song has outed Radha clearly.

> [*Embarrassed, Radha doubles down.*

Flute's last enchanting song, young lady's, nailed You to the spot;
You're tearful - I demand absurd dissembling's best forgot!

Vish. She won't persist, Lalita – tune's a deadly, tantric spell;
Lights the fires of emotion, it is modesty's death knell;
A mystical pronouncement certifies: love meant to be!

Radha. [*Still affected.*] Insidious - sakhi - truth is, the flute's much worse than deadly!
Monstrous flute - your songs are barbed as wretched Cupid's arrows!
They don't kill, but maim - instate a life of hobbling sorrows;
Slaying is what you should do – it really would be kinder.

Krishna. [*Expectant.*] Here's Rangini-the-deer, which means, sakhe - we've Radhika!
Radha-deer – deer-Radha – like the fabled deer-in-moon.

> [*Scrutinising.*

Ah. It is the moon's deer. My mistake – I spoke too soon;
Moon heading My way's no deer - indeed's – entirely spotless. [*Checks.*
It's Radharani's smiling face illuminating Us!

> [*Presses forward.*

Madhu. [*Jovially.*] Woah, friend – don't lose Your marbles, now – hold onto that decorum!
Those savvy girls have addled You – sharp craftiness about them;
Keep a grip on Your emotions - I will save You presently!

> [*Holds Krishna's hand.*

Krishna. Yes, thank you. With fair Radha, it's so hard to keep it steady;
Appreciate the help, My friend - [*They continue.*] My ardour overwhelms Me;
Galvanic how She's decorated so exquisitely;
She is the ashoka flower, My heart's the bumble-bee!

Radha. [*Observing Krishna sidewise. Aside.*] Here's the one, the youth puts paid to all good sense in Me;
Jasmine crown, flower pendants – smartly dressed to enervate;
When, through Krishna's eyes, His feelings speak – how's one think straight?

Vish. [*Smiles.*] You do not need to try a jot – here's pure infatuation,
Just Your perfume's enough to manage Krishna's subjugation!
And as the all-out victor - You don't need to battle on.

Radha. And, all you do is mock Me with uncalled-for provocation!
Don't want to be your friend – I have My one true friend, Lalita. [*Crosses to Lalita.*
Help me, sakhi, please – come on! Kanhaiya's getting nearer!
I can't hide in the forest, and My duty's to prevent Him!

Lal. [*Amused.*] He wrapped You in His scarf and now you'd rather we repel Him?
Look - I guarantee one thing - that no one else will touch You!

Krishna. [*Delighted.*] Beautiful! [*Approaches Radha.*

Lal.   [*Crossing proudly to block Him.*] Now, prince, don't You be frivolous – I warn You!
She's my treasured friend.

Krishna.   [*Smiling.*] Lalita, we aren't in the village;

Different place the forest – mean, out here, you have no leverage.

Lal. Kanhaiya, You'd scare a lightweight, but You're dealing with Lalita!

[*Radha nervously eyes Krishna, sidewise.*] What is it with Your nerves, Radhe? You're right beside Lalita.

Radha. Em, we've got our flowers, Lalita, so, let's go back to the river.

Krishna. Stealing noon-flowers, heartless girl, and now off to the river?!
[*Blocking Radha.*] You know the hill's obstructed by a hedging of bamboo?
Rocky! Also steep – not sure it's practical for You!
What's the best way to the river? One a little less frustrating?

Radha. [*Confident front.*]I've got a task to do, prince - so You can't blame Me for going;
Your mother - Gokool's queen - decides the schedule that we follow.

Krishna. What are You afraid of, Radhe? You're quite free to go.
[*Willing an embrace.*] I was happy to present You with that lovely scarf You're wearing.

Radha. [*Pleasing frown.*] Lalita inspires in Me a yen for righteous living;
This isn't right, Kanhaiya. You don't treat me - seriously.

Krishna. Lalita – any treat She wants to have's My foremost duty. [*Opens His arms invitingly.*

Lal. [*Moving Radha behind her.*] But, not a hug! And what is strange is how You don't know better!
You're widely praised, why, goodness me - You're Gokool's prince, Kanhaiya.

Madhu. Alright – Vrindavan forest is my good friend's forest, yes?
And you can come and take His flowers, and, frankly, leave a mess!

Krishna. Yes - count their takings, sakhe – things are not going so fairly.
Straight swap. As many necklace jewels as flowers got out of Me.

Madhu. All done, my friend – for each red flower we confiscate a ruby;
For every white flower, they'll need give a diamond or a pearly.

Krishna. You know, in fact, sakhe – I think My flowers are underpriced;
I'd like a fairer rate.

Madhu. [*Ministerial tone.*] Please don't forget that I'm a priest!
You be content with what you've got.

Krishna.   You're boss – I'll go along.

Lal. [*Smiles.*] That's good advice, young priest.

Vish.   [*Apparent alarm.*] Kanhaiya - careful!

Krishna. Why, what's wrong?

Vish. My dear friend's riled, so, mind Yourself! Beware counter-attack!
With Radhika, if chips are down – there is no turning back!

Krishna. [*Smiles.*] That's fine by Me, young lady – I shall deal with Her - no fear!
This rabid siren's jewels are Mine – they don't belong to Her! [*Advances on Radha.*

Lal. [*Menacingly.*] I wouldn't - not if I were You, Kanhaiya – don't touch Radhika!

Krishna. Lalita's exploded, sakhe – I don't recognise her!

Radha. Will you calm down, my friend! [*Embraces Lalita.*

Krishna.　　　　[*Aside to Lalita*] Lalita – you can't not agree!

Lal. Alright, what's *my* reward?

Krishna.　　　　[*Smiling.*] Lalita, fair play – now, let's see ...
Well, fighting Radha's out, but we could still fight - you and Me?

Lal. [*Turning her back.*] You really have a nerve!

Krishna.　　　　　　I'm saying – just tell Me the fee!

Lal. My friend needs her Sun-god flowers, so will You let Her be.
Long's She has the flowers She wants, prince, we've a kind of treaty.

Krishna. [*Smiles.*] Very fair, Lalita. [*Proceeds - Radha protests.*] Hey – what's going on? Not serious?!
　　　　　　　　　[*Reaches for Radha's necklace.*

Lal. [*Sly smile.*] Of course You have to wait, prince – She's got Sun-god temple Service,
You'd need a sacred bath, yourself, to take the jewels from Her.

Krishna. In case it wasn't obvious, dear, I do not need to bother;
I've had a sacred bath – I'm fully bathed in perspiration!

Lal. [*Whispers to Radha.*] It's not safe, Him getting angry in this desolate location.
If we're going to keep our jewels, sakhi – we'd better stay agree'ble.

Madhu. [*Gloating.*] No need worry, girls! [*Skips.*

Radha.　　　　　　　I'm sorry – I'm due at the temple!
Your casualness surprises Me, Lalita.

Madhu.   Temple-goers?
We too've a kind of worship - though, it's more intense, is ours;
Yes, you're not the only ones who're seraphic, Radhike.
    Vish. What kind's that, sir?
    Madhu.   Profound meditation, you might say;
In the groves – our holy temples - sacred sound's what we revere;
The chink of ankle bells approaching us is all we wait to hear!

                              [*Everyone smiles.*
[*Flattering.*] Your smile is very winning, pretty girl, you understand;
The cowherd of the groves, here, with the lotus in his hand;
Though wilful as an elephant – and as majestic too -
Is rooted to the spot, by that pert smile of lovely You!
    Krishna. And by Your violet-like enchantment - how You move just like a swan.
You're as dazzling as the forest, now the monsoon rains have gone.
Adorning You's to celebrate the wonder of this autumn!
    Madhu. Well, I'm blessed - the peacocks know exactly when you need them!
To decorate His Radha, Krishna needs some fancy feathers!
Fresh new peacock plumes with glist'ning moons in rainbow colours!
    Krishna. Feather tiara coming up - the peacocks did mind-read Me;
Let's gather! [*They go to collect plumes.*
    Radha. This is troubling. Lalita – cover for Me!
Boy's gone – I'm going to slip into this bower of ashokas.
                              [*Enters an ashoka grove.*

Krishna. This fine crown of peacock feathers, sakhe, is Radhika's.

[*Walks back.*] Lalita, where's your dear friend?

Lal. She's gone home – She did. It's true.

Krishna. Indeed, my sprite - that nice? You really think you're clever, don't you? [*Encouraged - He thinks He sees Her.*

Instantly – you see, My dear friend – yes! What glorious beauty! [*Heads off.*

Madhu. [*Amused.*] Are You sure You're alright, sakhe? Last typhoon turn You funny?

That's yellow pollen there!

Krishna. [*Checking.*] It is? It is! Good grief, too right, sir!

[*Changes direction.*] Her kunkum's just the same, you see. No, wait, sakhe - I see Her!

Madhu. [*Claps, laughs.*] Can't be helped – obsession, my friend - autumn blooms – all Radha!

Krishna. [*Drawing a blank.*] Violets? [*Observes Lalita, sidewise.*] Please help Me out. Oh, please do, fair Lalita!

Asking. Please. You've had your fun - I know you like to test Me.

Lal. You can ask Vishakha, handsome - knows as much as me. [*Curls a brow at Vishakha.*

Krishna. [*Notes signal. Aside to Madhumangala.*] Sakhe - a tacit signal from Lalita to Vishakha!

The burflower tree grove, eh?! Now I have no doubt whatsoever!

[*Confident smile.*] I know You're in there, precious – do come out the little dell.

[*No Radha. Smiles.*] A brilliant trick, Lalita – all your skills are working well.

Madhu. I'll get Radhika for You, friend.

Krishna. [*Encouraged.*] Thank goodness. Thank you, sakhe!
Lalita's unreliable – but you do what you say.

 Madhu. Of course I do.

 Krishna. [*Trusting.*] Come on, then, sakhe.

 Madhu.   Do do what I say.
But, for a price. [*Krishna gives him His jasmine garland.*]
And, so - for You ... [*Gives a leaf with 'Radha' written on it.*]

 Krishna. [*Smiles.*] That's nice. It's lovely, sakhe.
See or hear a true-love's name, the heart goes turning cartwheels;
A sweetheart's name intensifies and seals the love one feels! [*Surprised by a flowering ashoka tree to His right.*
My angel has a unique, and unusual sense of humour.
Ashokas, at this time, are really not supposed to flower;
Unless touched by a damsel – makes them bloom, no matter what;
The scent is drawing clouds of humming bees to this fine spot.
[*Delighted to spy Radha.*] What happened to You, precious?

 Radha. [*Apparently fractious.*] Make Me worry. Yes You do!
You found me out unfairly – now I can't escape from You.

 Krishna. I'm a pundit – 'course I found You – that's the reason I'm in charge.

 Lal. Oh, You're in charge? Allow me to remind You, Maharaja;
The god who You impressed one time - You being oh-so-clever -
Just goes on praising Radhika's amazing charm forever!
And the hill You lifted up – that was surprising – yes, it's true;
But one glance from my dear friend and She's full control of You!

Krishna. Now Lalita, My opinion is, your words are somewhat empty;
I shall hide – and when *I* do – then, none of you will find Me.

All. Right – You're on!
Krishna.   The tamal-grove's the place where I will vanish;
Stone's throw from here - the glossy foliage very Me - blue-blackish!

                    [*Exeunt Krishna and Madhumangala.*
Lal. Won't take any time at all, just hang on, Radha sakhi;
Spread out to find Kanhaiya, so we scout the wood entirely.
Radha. Alright, sakhi.

                [*They separate. Radha reaches the tamal-grove.*
[*Musing.*] Be a sport ... I bet He's sensed Me coming;
It is the place – somewhere near here. Kanhaiya, where're You hiding?
[*Walking.*] You deer know - Krishna's music's gone and done something to you,
Your mouths, though full of grass, don't work. Quite unable to chew!
[*Circumspect, continues.*] Now, when birds aren't flying, and the vines aren't wet with nectar;
I know I'm close to bumping into peacock-plume crowned Krishna.
[*Goes left.*] Indeed, I'm very sure He ambled by this way with flute;
Listless bees aren't supping, and there's parrots off their fruit;
Then, deer foregoing tasty leaves? No shadow of a doubt!
[*Continues.*] The tamal-grove – aha! [*Looks up.*] It's soundless. Monkeys all about;

I wonder what they're watching from their perches in the trees?

___What a mansion-of-a-grove – so calm – and curiously at ease.

Re-enter KRISHNA.

Krishna. [*Aside.*] Love has made Her heart become a Krishna-seeking compass;

I need to keep completely still, or that heart's going to find Us. [*Stands still.*

Radha. [*Spots Krishna, but pretends not to.*] No - not Kanhaiya – no.

Krishna. [*Aside.*] Thank goodness – phew, She didn't see me!

Radha. [*Smiling.*] Sapphire-pillar's what that is.

Krishna.   Great hiding place for Me!
No idea at all.

Radha.   It is a right-fine sapphire-piller!

Krishna. [*Delighted. Aside.*] Near pitch-dark, it is. Come closer - clueless girl, come closer.

Radha. [*Smiling.*] A Chandravali-beauty seems reflected in this pillar...

Krishna. [*Smiling. Aside.*] No cluelessness about that very dry, sarcastic humour. [*Comes out.*

___Chandravali's inalienably, always ever in Me;
That's to say, Radhika's supernatural lunar-beauty!

Radha. It's you! But, that makes sense, of course - not curious at all!

Krishna. Not funny – and You are going to join me - it's My call;
The scholar-tree grove's bouquet's grand – its pollen's deep as snow.

[*They go to a scholar-tree grove.*

Lal. Vishakha, wait – you see? Our friend is with Kanhaiya – no?
His footprints there, and Radha's there – of course, next to each other!

Vish. [*Following footprints.*] Footprints facing is embracing. Lagging there means banter;
Even footprints – sweet talk, see? Our sakhi's 'longside His?
So, now we know. We are apprised by Radha-Krishna paces!

Krishna. Listen, precious – can you hear? The chink of anklets? Faintly?
Stay very quiet.

Vish. So dense - this wood's just stuffed with bushes, sakhi;
I really do not know how that girl found Kanhaiya so quickly!

Lal. Why not? It's just a question of what pleases one the most;
A mango tree in bloom becomes an instant cuckoo-host!

Krishna. They're here, your friends – but, just pretend You haven't found Me, precious. [*Disappears.*

Lal. [*Cheerily approaching.*] Sakhi? So, where's the prince?

Radha. [*Smiling.*] Indeed – eluded all of us!

Lal. [*Candid smile.*] Really, betel-free lips? My, oh my, but You are careless!
Lost Your sense of dress? Now, where's the prince? It's time to tell us!
Don't You think a Gokool girl should excercise decorum?

Krishna. [*Re-emerging.*] You're right, Lalita, your friend here's an outright harum-scarum!
I put Myself first.

Lal. You can't abandon this nice gopi!

Krishna. But, I have to avoid Her, dear, She goes too far for Me!

[*Dramatically.*] This nice gopi scratches – sharp nails! That – was my plume crest!

Now look at it! My garland ruined – know what tops the rest?

That mask of innocence with which the girl denies it all!

Radha. [*Embarrassed.*] When it comes to playing victim, You've a rotten lot of gall …

Madhu. [*Off-stage.*] Jatila - but it is!

Radha. [*Alarmed.*] What!? No! The wicked crone - can't stay!

[*Exeunt Radha, Lalita and Vishakha.*

Madhu. [*Off-stage.*] Scholar-tree grove pollen – my, it does appear that way!

Just like Jatila's dusty locks - an uncanny resemblance!

Krishna. [*Exaggeratedly.*] Why's Pollen like Jatila's hair a thing you must announce?!

The boy really torments me - I need friends with better sense!

[*Exit.*

ACT VII.

Golden Goddess.

Vrin. Ah - the bur-tree blossom perfume, steady on the breeze.
Now the rainy season's over, my lush forests can't be quiet -
Potty peacocks. Jasmine-inspired bees all on a riot!
[*Distracted off-stage.*] Looks like serious talking here in Paurnamasi's garden;
What's Abhimanyu want from her? I'll stay a while and listen.

Enter PAURNAMASI *and* ABHIMANYU.

Paurna. Abhimanyu, dear – what's brought you this time of the morning?
Abhi. I've come to seek permission, noble lady.
Paurna.   It's regarding?
Abhi. Radha's leaving for Mathura.
Paurna. [*Disquieted.*] For ... ? And what's the call for this?
Abhi. Well - Radha and Kanhaiya - both. They're equally remiss;
More and more familiar.
Paurna.   Really? Who's said this, my son?

Abhi. My best friend, Govardhan.

Paurna. My dear – is he one to rely on?
Abhimanyu, question who exactly you're believing!
Can you trust someone who's loyal to Mathura's evil king?

Abhi. It's widely known what's going on – and that deserves a mention.

Paurna. My son, try and be patient, please. Don't let yourself be driven!
Let me explain.

Abhi. Alright.

Paurna. The truth may shock you, actually:
Mathura's king's obsessed - obsessed, with Radha's unique beauty;
Fixated like a hungry tiger stalking out its prey;
And you may be complicit, sir – helping him have his way!

Abhi. Dear lady, my friend Govardhan is clever with the king;
He has his ear, if he did not, then yes - we should be worrying.

Paurna. [*Considers anxiously.*] You're getting involved with folk who do not like Gokoola!
You're uncle to Gokoola's queen - a great uncle to Krishna!
Things are going well, it's better we make an agreement.

Abhi. Tell me what to do.

Paurna. My dear, I know how you're intent;
If you think the rumours genuine, not provocative lies;
Proceed, but only based on what you see with your own eyes.

Abhi. Alright. I like the idea ma'am.

Paurna. You are a gentleman.
May your herds keep on expanding!

Abhi. Hope to be like Govardhan;
His good wife Chandravali is a devotee of Gauri;

That's why their herds increase – ha - is my mother on at me!

'Radha should worship goddess Gauri! Get Her to the temple!'

    Paurna. Excellent - the way ahead! It will prove very fruitful;

And I'll remind Radhika.

    Abhi.   Noble lady – you're too kind!

                                           [*Exit.*

    Vrin. [*Approaching.*] Namas te, good lady!

    Paurna.   [*Hand-blessing.*] Bless you, dear – what's on your mind?

You're always up to something - will you tell us what's going on?

The latest Radha-Krishna news from autumn Vrindavan.

    Vrin. Extraordinary thing it is - the prince and Radha's love;

Indeed, it has become the thing we can't stop talking of;

Only time you stop is when the wonder of it gets you!

    Paurna. [*Gratified.*] Vrinda, dear – there's no surprise – since Krishna is Lord Vishnu,

Radhika and Krishna incarnating gives us purpose;

Real purpose to Cupid – whose work's generally so pointless!

Now, you say - I'd like to know what brings you to the village?

    Vrin. Appointed to a lovely task - a ritual of homage;

I hope to catch Lalita, noble lady.

    Paurna.   Why exactly?

    Vrin. A rendezvous occasion at the shrine of goddess Gauri;

Krishna's had me ensure the shrine courtyard's looking grand;

His lover shall have garlands and a lotus for Her hand.

    Paurna. Good to take advantage - it's always observed this way;

Romantic day for lovers, is this festive holiday;

The perfect day to give one's sweetheart quantities of flowers.

Gurantees her life's blessed, that on her all fortune showers!

    Vrin. This Maina bird broadcasted that in front of all the gopis -

And naturally, most assumed the day is Radharani's -

Fact all the gopis heard - they were all there along the byway;

But would you know it - Padma pipes up in that saucy way!

Claims that Chandravali's going to be the special one!

Saying any other girl will have to bite their tongue!

She added much disdain with daring looks aimed at Lalita.

    Paurna. [*Smiles.*] Gracious ...

    Vrin. Mind, Lalita kept composure, smiled, and affably ignored her.

No matter. Everything's arranged – we're going to find Radhika;

Lalita went to get Her - did she set off at a pace!

Here she is. At last. O-oh. Is she making a face?

Enter LALITA.

    Lal. Vrinda, now I know Padma was right to be so brassy;

Perhaps we shouldn't go!

    Paurna.   My dear – what happened? Will you tell me?

    Lal. Don't think it'll help, though, noble lady – seems it's fate.

Paurna. I'd like to hear, my dear - whatever's happened you must state.

Lal. [*Teary-eyed.*] Well, Radha gifted Kanhaiya a perfect flower garland;
With flowers sewn on a golden thread - I can't believe what happened!
I saw that Padma had it - Krishna'd given it to her!
Was in her hair!

Paurna.   It doesn't sound right. Gave the flowers to Padma?
That would give her the idea it's Chandravali's day!

Vrin. No – I know the story.

Paurna.   What's the story, Vrinda? Say!

Vrin. That garland-gift was taken - while Kanhaiya went to swim;
Was left out on a burflower tree, and Padma stole it from Him!
She told Him a sudden gust of wind swept it away;
Kakhati, the monkey's, the informer – by the way.

Lal. Goodness me – that true?

Vrin.   I swear the gopi's underhanded!

Lal. Ah, so - in Krishna's company, the garland-gift gets hid,
But, front of me, the thief waves it around - and so she did!

Paurna. Lalita, Padma's strategy has been well calculated,
Bent on her friend Chandravali getting to the temple;
Doing pretty well.

Vrin.   It's true, good lady – she's a hurdle;
Made things very awkward now – it could get complicated!

Enter VISHAKHA.

Vish. No, Vrinda – on the contrary – it's time we celebrated!

Vrin. Celebrate ... ?

Vish.   Chandravali, poor thing has been diverted!
Her guardian, Karala – has specifically stated -
That such a holiday dictates where any bride shoud be -
Right by her husband's side!

Lal.   [*Elated.*] Vishakha – that's good news to me!
Let's away!

Paurna.   Let's go. Now, Vrinda – Radhika is worried;
With Abhimanyu on the war path, it's for sure, She's being harried;
She'll need some reassuring, any luck, all will be fine.

Vrin. Very good – 'til later. We'll bring Krishna to the shrine;
Take Radha and Vishakha to the clove-grove in the yard!

                [*Exeunt Paurnamasi and Vishakha.*

Lal. [*Walking on the way to Gauri's temple.*] What's going on, my friend? This is becoming a charade -
That's Padma and Shaivya!

Vrin.   Think Vishakha was mistaken?
Not possible! [*Continuing. Reflects.*] Let's wait for Paurnamasi to catch up, then;
We're very keen, sakhi, but Radha's getting here's in doubt;
We've certainly made tracks, so we have time - we'll wait about.
Let's stay by the river.

                [*Exeunt Vrinda and Lalita.*

Enter PADMA and SHAIVYA.

Padma.   Sakhi Shaivya, you're depressed?

Shaiv. A prize thing snatched away, Padma – it's no surprise I'm stressed.

Kar. [*Off-stage.*] Chandravali to Govardhan! And then back here – you hear?
I want to see her covered in flower garlands, Padma, dear!

Shaiv. Thanks, noble Karala - that has really made my day!
Well? You heard her, Padma.

Padma. Did - was good to hear her say;
Properly encouraging!

Shaiv. You've lost me there, my friend.

Padma. Come, now – where is golden goddess Gauri's shrine positioned?
By Govardhan hill! What did you think Karala meant?
Our dear friend's husband, Govardhan? I think that would be torment!

Shaiv. You're a clever one, my friend! Let us get Chandravali!

Padma. She's on her way, in fact, expect she's almost there already!
I started her off – we'll catch her up. [*They speed off.*

Shaiv. Oh – where's the dress?
To offer to the goddess, Padma – where's ... ?

Padma. Madhu's the dress.

Shaiv. I can't deny that I'm still anxious 'bout our competition.

Padma. Oh, really, they won't bother us - they're full of consternation;
Made sure they saw this garland on me - foes faded away!

[*Shaivya embraces Padma.*
The temple courtyard looks divine, it's all going our way!
Kanhaiy and Chandravali's much-awaited rendezvous!

Kakhati. [*Off-stage.*] The temple courtyard looks divine, it's all going our way!
Kanhaiy and Chandravali's much-awaited rendezvous!

Shaiv. Sakhi, that monkey's out of ordermaking fun of you!
I do not like Kakhati's voice!

Padma.   [*Smiling.*] Hey, monkey! Hey there, wuss! You watch out, or I'll torch your mouth!

Kakhati.   [*Off-stage.*] Look you – you don't mind us! Your home is empty, Padma – going to take care of the butter!

Shaiv. She'll eat it, sakhi. No!

Padma.   She won't – she'd have to face Karala. [*Continuing, they hear Subal singing.*]
Look, leaning on his staff - there's Subal pausing by that tree.

Shaiv. [*Walking.*] And look there, by the little lake - it's Chandravali, sakhi!

Padma. There's our noble princess; smiling sweetly as a flower;
Our Chandravali's come across the one only Prince Krishna!

Enter CHANDRAVALI *and* KRISHNA.

Krishna. [*Blocking pathway.*] These eyes, you see, are bees. You are their honey, My beloved!

Chandra. Do let me through. I must get to the shrine that's up ahead!
There's worship to be done.

Krishna.   [*Smiling.*] I'm fairly sure you're pleased to see Me;
Your watery eyes, 'mongst other things, give that idea to Me;

Your dropped shawl's probably my seat – what gentile
etiquette!

Padma.& Shaiv. [*Arriving.*] Can go another way, sakhi.
If this way won't permit.

Chandra. [*Turns.*] Friends – I'm glad to see you!

Krishna.   [*Aside.*] Strange . Her being
here's surprised Me;
On My way to Radha. Not expecting Chandravali!

Padma. [*Aside to Krishna.*] Yes, handsome, Padma
heard Your wish , uhuh - I comprehend;
And bringing Chandravali was quite easy, in the end;
I like to be creative.

Krishna. [*Aside.*] Yes, I see. And well done you!
Nothing wrong delivering a meaning number two.
No harm done. __Sakhi – Krishna appreciates you dearly!

Padma. You may now take Chandravali to the shrine
of goddess Gauri!

Krishna. [*Aside.*] Won't do for Radhika to find us there
with Chandravali;
Lucky Chandra's easy going... and a delight to make happy...
__Chandravali sakhi - O divine, unblemished beauty!
Do you know - when I'm without you, I don't feel completely
Me?
[*They begin strolling.*] How the forest is enchanting –
would you not say, gentle one?

Padma. [*Sees the deer Suranga.*] That's Krishna's
fawn, Suranga, friend – quick – look - it'll be gone!
Rangini's mate, that is.

Krishna. [*Nervously listening. Aside.*] Must be Rangini
drew him hither. [*Cry of Rangini.*
And there's the doe! Wherever there's Rangini, there's
Radhika!

Padma. Where's Suranga darting off to?

Krishna. [*Aside.*] Obviously, it's Gauri's shrine;
Right – I'd best stay here, then - this lakeside will do just fine.

Padma. This lotus-lake reminds me of the way things are in Gokool;
Where lotus-girls are capsized on the waves of passion's pool.

Krishna. Where lotus flowers enjoy the light that's shining down upon them!
So much so, they're super-fragrant - bees cannot resist them;
You, Chandra, are most certainly, perfect-lotus-flower-like!

Shaiv. Dear me - your perfect lotus-flower's wilting – it looks like.

Padma. [*Gestures to moon.*] The Krishna-moon shines dimly, for the most part – that is why;
Don't forget, she has a sun 'pon whom she *can* rely!

Krishna. The problem's not the moon, Padma - if this flower's out of sorts;
It could be due to such a thing as shadowy, dark thoughts!

Chandra. [*Looks up, smiles.*] I'd like to say, while some flowers find bee-fickleness amusing;
Jasmine doesn't like it – nectar tears display her feeling.

Krishna. You know what, my angel – that there Bur-flower tree in view?
Serenaded by the bees, so grand? That reminds me of you;
Fanned by whisking cow-tails with due pomp and ceremony!

Chandra. I would say Lalita is Vrindavan Forest's beauty!

Re-enter VRINDA *and* LALITA.

Lal. [*Looking worriedly ahead.*] We really have a problem now!

Vrin. We do - it's very puzzling;
Karala's got an iron will that's just not worth resisting,
How's Padma brought Chandravali? Must be something I missed.

Lal. Got to prize Kanhaiya out, sakhi – well then, strategist?

Vrin. I'm not sure - she loves Him very much, does Chandravali;
To get Krishna away from her - it's not going to be easy.

Lal. Radharani's love's heroic – Chandravali's isn't;
Chandravali's love would hide with Radharani's present!

Vrin. Yes - I know. But, still, we cannot be uncivil, sakhi;
Bit tricky getting Krishna out.

Lal.   Alright, that's as may be -
You have to find the answer, Vrinda!

Vrin.   First, we'll go and join them;
Surmise the situation better. [*They approach their rivals.*

Shaiv. [*Aside to Padma.*] Padma, this is tiresome!
Lalita here, means Radha's at the shrine – it must be, sakhi!

Padma. And what? No way they can get rid of our dear Chandravali.

Lal. [*Arriving.*] Chandravali, we're worried 'bout that lovely doe, Rangini;
The fawn she loves is unconcerned that she loves him intensely;
He's dallying with other does, and living on a whim;
She should keep to herself – he's barely thought of her this autumn!

                          [*Chandravali shows surprise.*
Krishna. [*Aside*] Lalita refers to Me.
                          [*Observes Chandravali. Deliberates.*
                          __Lalita – less meddlesome!

You don't know Suranga's heart. You want to know about him?
He yearns for her, you tell that doe - her eyes command his being!

Padma. [*Aside to Krishna.*] Your favourites are here, Kanhaiya – sure You won't be staying;
Go, if You will, here's second-rate – go on – why need stay longer?

Krishna. [*Ambiguous.*] I don't like all the meddling, friend – now, who do I prefer?

Padma. [*Audacious smile.*] Mind if I ask, Lalita? It is curious to me;
You, without Radhika – I'm surprised, sakhi - where's She?

Lal. It's not lake to thirsty elephant - it's elephant to lake!
Bees, who want a sip of him, are vexing things that take.

Padma. Just what is the pretty thing that's most loved by Kanhaiya?
Shaivya knows the secret, and so she will give the answer.

Shaiv. It's Chandravali, sakhi!

Vrin.   [*Smiles.*] Naturally – and we all know it!
In fact, Kanhaiya's shield's a set of moons painted upon it.

Krishna. [*Chandravali shyly recedes. Aside.*] Bless her.

Lal.   Vrinda what name qualifies all shrines to Krishna?

Vrin. Radha - that's the one!

Krishna.   Both names for spring, yes - Radha-Krishna!

Padma. Let us hear the truth, Shaivya! What's Krishna all about?

Shaiv. [*Looking to the lake.*] The bee only likes lilies if the lotus flower's not out;
When he spots the lotus blooms, he bids lilies bye bye!

Padma. Of course - as stars remain a pleasing feature of night-sky,
But aren't of any int'rest once the waxing moon arrives.
Lal. [*Laughs.*] Radha's like the sun, dear one - what happens, then, at, sunrise?
All interest in the waxing moon's diminished in a trice!
Krishna. [*Smiling.*] Splitting hairs - fact is, in spring that all the flowers smell nice!
Vrin. [*Smiles.*] Yes, all flowers enchant the bee in spring, in their own way;
But jasmine mostly, Jasmine is the name was given Radhe!
Padma. [*Flouncing off.*] Inane circus, Chandravali! We've important temple service!
Krishna. Padma, why discourage Chandravali, when she loves us?
Interrupting flowers is for weeds! Say, like ... Karala...?

Enter KARALA.

Kar. Ah, yes! Just a minute, there! [*Everyone turns.*
Shaiv. [*Aside to Padma.*] It's one thing or another! How's granny got on to us?
Kar.   The best in town, that monkey!
Perhaps a butter-addict, but she speaks the truth to me.
                         [*Padma gives Shaivya a horrified look.*
Lal. [*Aside.*] Kakhati, my dear primate, there'll be sugared-ghee for you!
Krishna. [*Aside to Chandravali.*] There's no way out, beloved. Fully trapped! What shall we do?
The hill's too steep to climb, this side you've well-behaved cow-herders;
Behind us there's no cover, then the wicked crone's before us!
Aren't spoilt for choice.

Chandra. [*Aside.*] O-oh - the angry harridan's hell-bent!

Kar. [*Flustered.*] Cobra eyes! You're black as night! And leering like a serpent!
Heading good, religious girls along the road to ruin!
[*Trembles. Widens eyes.*] I do not think You've understood the peril that You're in -
Whose wife is this, Kanhaiya? Hm? Might as well get it right;
A giant of a wrestler, oh, and partial to a fight -
Mathura's king and he are both alike - nastily similar!

Krishna. Go on, dear Karala.

Kar.   Just who do you think you are!
Cow king! Haha! Delude Yourself then, miles out in the forest;
When You come to the real king's court, let's see You self-impressed!
You're going to feel so tiny!

Krishna.   Dear Karala, please believe Me -
Seeing Chandravali makes Me anxious - factually!

Kar. [*Rounding on Chandravali.*] What got into you? You're always, always in these bowers!
Since childhood. Finding ways to meet Kanhaiya here for hours!
Throw virtue to the wind, for what? Those lips? Who else has kissed Him?
A thousand daft girls – oh, what now? You're worried? Am I fearsome?
Stay where you are!

Lal.   Good lady, it's not she, or He, to blame!
Why sun and the horizon meet each evening is the same;
An independent agent is promoting the encounter -

Twilight's promoting sunset, while this trysts arranged
by...

    Kar.   By Padma!!
Thank you, daughter. [*Menacingly.*] Oh, you slave! That's
you – fixer! Home-wrecker!
Pretty free and easy, eh? Well, not so any longer!

                                       [*Brandishes her staff.*

    Padma. [*Cowering.*] I don't understand, good lady –
we did what you told us!

    Vrin. [*Aside.*] Ah - 'course you did - you're Padma, the
creative genius!

___Wait, good lady! Sometimes this girl's common sense is
nil,

'Course you meant the husband, but the silly girl thought
hill!

Don't bother chastising her!

                                     [*Karala lowers staff.*

    Padma.   [*Aside.*] It's pay-back time, Lalita!
You just wait and see - I'm heading right now for Jatila!

                                             [*Exit.*

    Kar. [*To Chandravali.*] Come with me, you forest
vagrant!

                   [*Exeunt Karala, Chandravali and Shaivya.*
    Krishna. [*Sighs.*] You've a lot up your sleeve, Vrinda!

    Vrin. She's waiting. Gauri's temple's hosting Your
lovely Radhika;

Here's some fragrant flowers of Hers She wanted me to
give You.

    Krishna. [*Very glad to receive them.*] I'm coming,
Vrinda. Check the cows, and then I'll be there too.
You two go on ahead!

                                             [*Exit.*

Vrin. [*Walking.*] And here's my forest's best burflower tree.
[*Approaches tree.*] Krishna loves burflowers - you blooms, you are extremely lucky,
The famous jewel upon His chest's lack-lustre next to you!

[*They arrive at the courtyard by Gauri 's temple.*]

Lal. Paurnamasi and Vishakha, Vrinda – there you are – the two,
They're in the mango grove!

Vrin. That's right – and, look what I have spied!
The goddess of Fortune - or, p'haps Beauty personified?
No, it is Radhika - the embodiment-of-love.
[*Ponders.*] Of course it is - more pretty than the great goddess above!
Alike, though, in the way She holds and twirls a lotus flower;
Has one in Her braids as well - one set upon Her ear.

Paurna. [*Off-stage.*] Here He comes - the Queen of Gokool's precious, darling son;
With flute - red clay-marks gleaming - aye - our full attention's won!
Hyacinths behind His ears, plume-crowned, and Bur-flowers on.

Lal. The Lady spies Kanhaiya?

Vrin. Yes, Lalita – back anon.
Peacock-plume provider's energised to do some dancing;
If Krishna's not in sight, sakhi, that bird has trouble breathing!

Lal. Ah – by the laurel trees, sakhi.

[*Sound of the flute.*]

Vrin. [*Delighted.*] The master of the cows.
Compliance is the thing the prince's magic flute endows;

The splendid pipe is what makes Him the quintessential cowherd!

Lal. Neither's seen the other yet, but Rangini's bestirred;
Kanhaiya's directed - to the clove trees He must go!

Vrin. She's cottoned on He's coming – Krishna's fragrance tells Her so;
Our gleeful gopi slips into the madhavi-grove, sakhi.
[*Scrutinising.*] Leaving Him a helpful set of footprints – way too easy!
One stealthy move, and Krishna's hand is over Radha's eyes!

Lal. Oooh – lotus-lash reprisal! Love for Krishna in disguise!

Vrin. Full on, half-baked protest as She struggles not to smile;
Unconvincing counteroffensive, Radhika- style;
Well, all in the open, friend, what use is Her pretending?
Radha loves the prince, and here, the great pretence is ending!

Lal. He needs to look out because She's not pulling her scratches!
Krishna doesn't seem displeased with those bright wounds of His.

Vrin. [*Laughs.*] Disastrous, Her mascara – red dye smeared - it's all but gone!
A lot of sweat and tears, our Radharani's sash's half-on:
You could even imagine She just might like to embrace Him!

Lal. Lost to the world, indeed, and - oh! The - madhavi grove's lost them!

Vrin. Our eyes are the bees enslaved to Radha-Krishna honey.

Lal. Flowers in the grove, but all the bees are going, sakhi!

Vrin. Naturally, same as us. The couple's left the arbour!

The bees cannot resist the divine couple's fine aroma.

Let's check the bower, shall we? Come. I'd like to go and see.

[*They enter the grove.*] Pearls are scattered, look – a shame about Her broken jewellery;

Enchantress's new garland doesn't look too clever either;

This flower-grove advertises some Prince Krishna striking theatre!

Lal. [*Astutely.*] Here's a thing - yes - here we have Their sweat-beads tinged vermilion -

Radha's lac and Krishna's saffron mixed – beautiful union!

Vrin. [*Impressed.*] Seems like yesterday when she was playing in the dust;

Had ribbons, newly pierced ears – I dare say, I am nonplussed;

Has Radha really put the never-conquered in His place!

Lal. [*Looks up.*] There's Radha and Krishna, Vrinda!

Vrin. 　　　　　　　　　　　　Flower-festival's showcase.

Let's hear Radha.

Radha. [*Off-stage.*] Yes - clove flowers. A lotus on My ear;

Excellent - the jasmine chaplet in place, handsome - here!

Make sure that it's not going to slip down from my head again;

Kadamba flowers round hips – alright – I think I'm ready, then!

You see? No gopi girl can say Krishna did not adorn me!

Vrin. [*Smiles.*] Prince looks very good, as well – wounded artistically;

Feathers, here and there, and drops of pearl-like beads of sweat;
Inebriating vision. One I'm sure not to forget.

Re-enter RADHA, *decorated with various flowers, and*
KRISHNA.

Krishna. Henna frills, for what? You've wavy curls like filigree;
Your eyes humble the renown of the lotus flowers' beauty;
Your pearls are simply pointless, nothing compares to Your smile;
Your beauty states it stridently - the extras aren't worthwhile.

Lal & Vrin. [*Approaching with flowers.*] More flowers, handsome - finish off the homage perfectly!

Krishna. [*Pleased to receive the blossoms.*] As I am often honoured, by fine folk inclined to Me;
As your devoted follower, My jasmines honour The!

[*Places blossoms on Radha.*

Kakhati. [*Off-stage.*] Just four o'clock - my, my - the cow herd's turning back already!
Let's hear it for the monsoon grass! A solid testimony!

Lal. Radhe, I'm going to pick the best bouquet of all - you'll see!
You wait.

[*Exit.*

Krishna. [*Aside to Vrinda, smiling.*] Now, my dear Vrinda – can I ask a little favour?
Monkey Kakhati - in the tree – I want to borrow her;
My new salvo is going to demand complicity.

Vrin. Of course.

Krishna. [*Crossing to Radha.*] And now. My own - My very dearest Chandrava...

[*Apparently muddled.*

Radha. [*Mortified.*] Sorry?
I didn't hear that right, because My ears would have exploded...

Vrin. [*Aside.*] Kakhati, you're tasked to say whatever Krishna wants said;
As I wave my wand, you'll know what He wants you to say!
[*Discreetly waves peacock-feather wand.*
__Don't turn away! Oh, now, sakhi ...

Krishna.   Oh, My dear Chandra - *naney*!
What's wrong?

Kakhati. [*Off-stage.*] Do not be fooled, lady - Lalita couldn't take it!

Radha. [*Sees Kakhati. Aside.*] Kakhati? 'Nough's enough! __Do not say any more about it!
Don't You try and drown out thunder with a little drum!

                [*Turns her back.*

Krishna. [*Aside to Vrinda.*] Intense and fiery Radha is a prodigy, and some!
The full-arched bow of Cupid's not as intense as Her brow.
[*Catching Radha's sari.*] __This here and now's our moment, angel – going so well, now!

Kakhati. [*Off-stage.*] No, no! No - do not fall for it! Insult to injury!
The Padma clan is laughing at us!

Radha.   [*Retreating.*] Vrinda - 'nough for me!
A laughing stock, am I? It's first one thing, then it's another;
Travesties at My expense – you tell Him not to bother!
And, tell Him not to play His flute and spoil vindictively!
It only needs be said that He's Chandravali's pet monkey!

Krishna. [*Smiling affably.*] Vrinda – please talk to Radha.

Vrin.   Radha – give Krishna a chance!
You know, it might be best if you don't take too strong-a stance.

Radha. [*Contemptuous.*] There's no point my being here!

[*Exit.*

Krishna.   Don't overdo it, Vrinda;
Don't want to get her all annoyed.

Vrin.   Well, put me in the picture!

Krishna. Vrinda, you and I are going to bring Radhika round;
Your savoire faire, and Me dressed up! The jolly venture's sound!

[*Vrinda smiles assent.*

Ah. Wondered 'bout the gold make-up - we certainly may need some.

Enter MADHUMANGALA.

Madhu. Gold paint and the most darling dress awaiting in the sanctum!
Courtesy of Padma, friend.

Krishna.   [*Very pleased.*] Now Vrinda, here's the thing:
We're sisters. Let us meet in Gauri's temple for some acting!

[*Exeunt Krishna and Madhumangala.*

Vrin. [*Walks a way, and spies the sakhis.*] Ah, the bouquet-pickers being exposed to the news;
Radha looks remorseful – clearly clueless it's a ruse.

Re-enter RADHA, LALITA *and* VISHAKHA.

Radha. Sakhi – I just couldn't stop this fiercely, deep disdain;
Was in no state to be appeased.
    Lal. So, Radhe – think again;
He'd not let slip another's name – not, even in a dream -
Believing in that hair-brained monkey – that's what's made you steam.
    Vish. Lalita, I tell you – it's those jealous girls – I bet you!
Spoiling things this way or that, is all they ever do.
    Lal. Should they see we're upset now, I guarantee they'd snicker;
Sneer, as well. They're quite a crew. It's what they're like, Vishakha.
    Radha. [*Aside.*] My friends are sadly right – so, what's the plan? What is the answer?
    Vrin. [*Approaching.*] Krishna wants His elder brother, Balaraam, Lalita;
I'm fetching Him.
    Lal. What for?
    Vrin. A stroll - take in the season's beauty.
    Vish. Could you give us a minute, Vrinda sakhi? 'Fore you hurry?
    Vrin. I'm going to be honest – rather not. Maybe talk later.
    Vish. Why?
    Vrin. You ask your friend there. Who was very rude to Krishna!
Upset Him ...
    Radha. [*With a sigh.*] Sakhi Vrinda – the way forward's down to you.
    Vrin. [*Apparently reproachful.*] But, what possessed You, crosspatch? I beheld a jealous shrew!

Gone. Unreachable, You were – and He'll go that way too!
Our sovereign prince is loved by many girls, and not just
You!
I don't know why You're sighing, friend.

    Lal. Know where Kanhaiya is?

    Vrin. In Gauri's shrine.

    Lal. And what's He ...?

    Vrin. He's relaxing with
a friend of His;
You know - Nikunjavidya.

    Lal, Vish & Radha. Who's Nikunjavidya, sakhi?

    Vrin. [*Laughs.*] Nikunjavidya? Don't you know her?
You young girls are funny!

    Lal, Vish & Radha. [*Meekly.*] It's true, though - we don't
know her, sakhi.

    Vrin. So, where've you been hiding?
Presides over the Banyan wood - astounded you've no inkling!
I thought that all the gopis did - sister to me, you know.

    Lal. Vrinda, without you, this problem isn't going to
go.

    Vrin. Suppose Nikunjavidya's party to all Krishna's
secrets...
No harm in dropping by. Alright, my friends - she's there
– so, let's!

                [*They walk to the shrine courtyard.*

    Radha. Gauri's temple. Shall we get Nikunjavidya out,
now?
Vrinda? Make a sign - go in and nod, or something - bow.

    Vrin. [*Peering in. Aside.*] Damsel by the door – oh,
what a glow – how very pleasing!
__Only her – the Banyan goddess – fixing up an earring.

    Lal, Vish & Radha. Now you just wait a minute -
Kanhaiya's peacock's in the courtyard!

Vrin. No-one's stopping you from looking! You owe me more regard.

Lal. Bird's got to've been asleep, friend – can't have seen Kanhaiya go.

Radha. Let's go inside, sakhi – Nikunjavidya's going to know.

> [*They enter the temple.*

Enter JATILA.

Jat. What a gem is gopi-Padma – priceless tidings out the blue!
Good fortune's in, she says to me – you'll see what's in for you!
Your son, Jatila's, like to get more cows than Govardhan!
So, Radhika's at Gauri's shrine – the worship is in hand...
She's made my son proud, after all – and I shall let Her know!

> [*Spots Radha's doe – Rangini - in temple courtyard.*

Padma, you dear - straight-dealing, just so honest. And ...O-oh!
The bird? Oh, no! It is! Kanhaiya's peacock's on the pillar!
Final straw! Understand now! My son'll deal with this!

> [*Exit, running.*

Radha. [*To Lalita and Vishakha.*] Do you see, my friends? We have a transcendental goddess!

Lal & Vish. Absolutely, sakhi. You can see why Krishna'd trust her.

Radha. Little nervous about asking. After all – first time I've met her. [*Is bashful.*

Krishna. [*Off-stage, as Nikunjavidya.*] Sister Vrinda, it appears that Radha cannot place Me;
Can't count the times that She's been made appreciable to Me.

Vrin. [*Aside.*] There's talent for you!

Radha.   Vrinda. Why d'you think she strikes
Me so?
Nikunjavidya captivates Me.

Vrin.   Yes? And why not so?
She appreciates You - much affection for You, sakhi.

Radha. [*Happily reassured.*] Nikunjavidya, would You
tell us where Your fellow-friend might be?

Krishna. [*Off-stage, as Niku.*] But, no-one knows, My
dear.

Lal. Nikunjavidya – tell us, sakhi!
We're His friends as well.

Krishna. [*Off-stage, as Niku.*] My child, a secret is a secret;
Like making gold from mercury - there's few know much
about it.

Vrin. [*To Radha.*] Ingratiate Her, Radhe - Niku's smile's
saying She wants you!

Radha. Nikunja, could You love Me as has Vrinda,
hitherto?

Krishna. [*Off-stage, as Niku.*] You're the gentlest-
looking gopi, one could ever hope to meet;
Why, dainty as a flower, from cooling face to lotus feet;
But, a core's still necessary to give strength, of course, I
know;
That's why You have a hard heart - the creator made You
so!

Radha. She's teasing, Vrinda. See? Her smile? All fine.
I will go over.

[*Exit.*

Vrin. Oh, dear me – greet Her properly. A hug,
Nikunjavidya!
The sakhi longs to be a friend - stop stalling gopi-lover!

Vish. There – Radhika's thrown Her arms around
Nikunjavidya.

They're getting on!

Radha. [*Off-stage.*] I'm due home very soon, beautiful lady;
I must make up with Krishna, and time's running out so quickly.

Lal. [*With consternation.*] Your sister's very loving with Radhika, Vrinda sakhi!

Vish. [*Suspicious.*] Your Nikunjavidya's ways are definitely manly!
Got to be more careful 'bout how sharp those nails She has are!

Vrin. [*Smiles.*] Don't be anxious, friend – love's way's are seldom not bizarre.

Re-enter RADHA.

Radha. [*Black-browed, shaken.*] You really took Me, Vrinda!

Vrin.   [*Laughing.*] Not so, friend – what are You saying?

Lal & Vish. [*Cheerfully.*] We *do* know Nikunjavidya after all, Vrinda – She's charming!

Re-enter JATILA *with* ABHIMANYU.

Jat. Abhimanyu – that's Rangini. And Kanhaiya's bird? You see?
Both of them in the courtyard!

Abhi.   Oh, yes. Mother, do I see!
When Balaraam returned the cows, Kanhaiya wasn't with Him!

Jat. The outlaws are within, my boy - Their perfumes have betrayed Them!

Abhi. I've been patient - Paurnamasi wanted that I wait.
It's Mathura for Radhika - before it is too late!

Jat. Only one way in, look - here - let's us get nice and near;

Get right up by the door. That's it. Can hear Them loud and clear.

Re-enter KRISHNA.

Krishna. [*Smiling. Female voice.*] You're asking the impossible, Radhe, on this occasion!

Radha. [*In jest.*] Dear goddess - pretty please ...

[*Abhimanyu bursts into the temple.*

Abhi. I think that someone lacks discretion!!
It's all over now, outlaw!

Krishna. [*Aside.*] Oh, precious - don't fall over!
Heavens - Abhimanyu's voice - the sound of him has floored Her!

Jat. [*Astonished, pointing.*] I see an apparition! Son - who's dazzling Gauri's chantry?

Abhi. [*Adding things up.*] It is the golden goddess, Ma – with Radha at her feet - see?
Upon my word it is the golden goddess - personally!

Krishna. [*Aside.*] I'll be bound! This goddess-outfit comes in very handy!

Lal & Vish. [*Excited.*] You said to invoke Gauri! You predicted she'd appear, sir!

Abhi. Vishakha, what's impossible? What can't Gauri grant Radha?

Krishna. [*Acting as goddess Gauri.*] Abhimanyu, my dear sir, an evil fate awaits you;
I'd help, but it is too, too late – there's nothing I can do!

Abhi. [*Worried.*] Fate? What fate, goddess?

Krishna. [*As goddess.*] Vrinda, I shudder to explain;
Please tell him.

Vrin. Abhimanyu, sir - Mathura's king's insane;
He's sacrificing humans, and tonight - he will axe you!

Jat. [*Bewildered.*] Mercy! Goddess – let my son live!

Radha.   [*Rising. Light-hearted.*] Goddess, please - we beg You!

Krishna. [*As goddess, smiling.*] I'm truly sorry, Radhe – but there is just no way round it!

Radha. O gopi-saviour – all You have to do's say 'so-be-it!'

Please – there is no point in life for Me without My lord!

Krishna. [*As goddess, smiling.*] Normally, Radhe, there's no request I must award;

I suppose I can't deny You - have your wish – with one proviso;

Keep worshipping Me! Stay in Gokool village – never go!

Abhi. [*Sigh of relief.*] Your kindliness is famous - You've my solemn guarantee;

I'll not take Radha to Mathura – She shall stay to worship The!

Jat. [*Embracing Radha.*] My girl – I'm saved!

Vrin. [*Addressing Abhimanyu.*] There's still something that needs be sorted out;

If a man rebukes a lady, his longevity's in doubt;

Goddess Gauri-the-judicial will decide what should be done.

Krishna. [*As goddess.*] Radhika's good fortune, Abhimanyu, lucky one;

To lose your faith in Her's not less than misbegotten rashness.

Abhi. I've been very foolish, but Subal's no help, goddess;

All primped up as Radha - and, alright - he's teasing mother;

But, it gets people talking, it's no joke - it isn't clever!

Lal. Great credit you still do have confidence, then, Abhimanyu.

Abhi. Let's get back to the house, Ma – got some unpacking to do!

[*Exeunt Jatila and Abhimanyu, with low bows.*
Lal & Vish. [*Tearfully clutching Radha.*] Brutes! Dear friend - so very nearly banished to Mathura!

Enter PAURNAMASI.

Paurna. [*Smiling broadly.*] You're beautiful. But so - good Lady of the Banyan arbour;
It's wonderful to see You!

Krishna. [*Crossing to her.*] Good to see you, holy lady!

Paurna. Yashoda's son, well done - bless You! I've renewed energy;
No more dismal thoughts of losing Radha any more.

Krishna. Radha's safe. No shadows – misfortune's been shown the door!
Everybody's happy - is there something else, good lady?

Paurna. [*Tearfully appreciative.*] Gokool-boy, there's nothing, but, then, since You're asking me;
Your pastimes in Vrindavan so beguile, there should be more!
Continue them with Radha, please? That, I'd be grateful for:
A taste for Radha-Krishna magic's easily acquired;
A brief encounter with it, and one's latent nature's fired;
So begins the reawakening of long-lost love for You!

Krishna. [*Smiling.*] Why, noble lady - I agree – as you say, so I do!
But, now, I must get home – way past the milking time already;
Can't bear seeing my parents anxious – have to keep them happy!

[*Exeunt.*

EPILOGUE.

The charm of Radharani and the genius of Krishna,
I trust, may draw attention from both, gentleman and
scholar;
I was thinking, as I came to write the last act of my
drama:
That thankfully, the gentle devotees of Lord Shree
Krishna,
Enhance what's good, and what is not - they somehow
rarefy;
An effect that's like how bright stars decorate the
midnight sky.
The year is fifteen thirty two, my work completed in
Vrindavan.

GLOSSARY.

avatar incarnation.
Bali a renowned king.
Brahma creator god.
chakora a bird said to live by moonlight alone.
chandravali a set of moons.
deer-in-moon as in, 'man-in-moon.'
dharma religion.
Diwali festival of lights.
Durga consort of Shiva.
Gauri a form of goddess Durga.
ghat bathing place.
Gokoola village in Vrindavan.
gopi cowherd girl.
gunja berries bright red jequirity berries.
hala friend.
Indra king of heaven.
jai hail!
Kamsa king of Mathura city.
Kanhaiya alternative for 'Krishna'.
Madhavi springtime flower.
Mathura city neighbouring Vrindavan.
meru name of a legendary golden mountain.
Narada sage among the gods.

puja worship.
Radha, Radhe, Radhika alternatives for 'Radharani'.
rasa dance a fervent dance.
Rambhoru name of a famously beautiful goddess.
Sachi-nandana Shree Chaitanya, the son of Sachidevi.
sakhe male friend.
sakhi female friend.
Sandipani Krishna's teacher.
Santanu a place near Gokoola.
Shiva god of end times, and patron to the arts.
shree 'his eminence.'
shriman venerable m.
shrimati venerable f.
Vrindavan Vrinda's forest.
Yamuna name of Vrindavan's river.
Yuthi a kind of jasmine.

* 9 7 8 1 9 1 5 9 9 6 9 8 5 *